"Bree?"

She gasped at the sound of her name and turned from the window.

Austin stood naked except for his pajama pants, which rode low on his hips, looking sexier than he had earlier that night.

"Yes?"

"Why aren't you in bed?"

His masculine scent reached out to Bree, sending her entire body into a heated tailspin.

"I thought you were sleeping," she said, trying to stay in control.

A slow smile touched his lips and her body tingled in response.

The erratic pounding in her chest returned.

Had it truly ever left?

"I couldn't sleep." He rubbed a hand over his face. "You should probably try to get some rest. We have an early flight in the morning."

Bree glanced down at her empty cup and came up with the perfect excuse to leave the living room. "I've finished my tea. Maybe sleep will come now."

When she walked past him, Austin reached out, taking the cup from her hand and placing it on the end table before wrapping a strong arm around her waist and pulling her to him.

His head lowered to hers.

Dear Reader,

For unmarried biological fathers, having the right to consent or object to the adoption of one's child is a huge issue. Imagine not knowing about that child until after the fact. In *Return to Me*, Austin DuGrandpre moves to Charleston for two reasons: to build a relationship with his father and to find his son.

My inspiration for this story was born out of an article I read about fathers in certain states having to prove paternity if they are not married to the mother.

I hope you will enjoy reading Austin and Bree's story in the third installment of The DuGrandpres of Charleston.

I love hearing from my readers, so please visit me on the following:

Twitter: www.Twitter.com/jacquelinthomas

Web: www.jacquelin-thomas.com

Email: jacquelinthomas@gmail.com

Blessings to you,

Jacquelin Thomas

RETURN
TO *Me*

JACQUELIN
THOMAS

HARLEQUIN®KIMANI™ ROMANCE

Recycling programs
for this product may
not exist in your area.

ISBN-13: 978-1-335-21668-7

Return to Me

Copyright © 2018 by Jacquelin Thomas

For questions and comments about the quality of this book please contact us
at CustomerService@Harlequin.com.

H HARLEQUIN®

™ www.Harlequin.com

Printed in U.S.A.

Jacquelin Thomas is an award-winning, bestselling author with more than fifty-five books in print. When not writing, she is busy catching up on her reading, attending sporting events and spoiling her grandchildren. Jacquelin and her family live in North Carolina.

Books by Jacquelin Thomas

Harlequin Kimani Romance

Five Star Attraction
Five Star Temptation
Legal Attraction
Five Star Romance
Five Star Seduction
Styles of Seduction
Wrangling Wes
Five Star Desire
Forever My Baby
Only for You
Return to Me

Visit the Author Profile page
at Harlequin.com for more titles.

Prologue

"*I* wish I'd never met you," she muttered as she ripped clothes from hangers, tossing them into a tattered suitcase.

"Jasmine, I'm sorry you feel that way," Austin Du-Grandpre responded. "The truth is that we're toxic together, so it's best to end things now."

A cold, congested expression settled on her face as she hurled a string of profanity back at him.

Jasmine was leaving town with her best friend, and Austin thought it was a good idea. They needed some separation. They had dated for two years and the relationship was tumultuous at best. For the past month, Jasmine had been pressuring Austin for a marriage proposal. When nothing came of it, she decided to give him an ultimatum—marry her or she would leave town and find a new man.

Austin chose the latter. Jasmine was free to start over with someone new. Perhaps she'd be much happier.

Her mouth took on an unpleasant twist as she shot daggers toward him with her eyes. "I can't believe I wasted all this time with you. I should've known better than to get involved with someone like you..."

Austin opened his mouth to utter a retort, but remained

silent. He would not allow himself to be baited into another argument with Jasmine.

"Did you ever love me?"

"That wasn't the problem."

She frowned with cold fury. "Then what is it? I'm not good enough to be your wife—the wife of a lawyer?" Jasmine folded her arms across her chest. "What? You wanna be with some snobby ivy league graduate...huh?"

"Jasmine, the problem is that you and I are not a good fit," Austin stated. "You can't go around starting fights with every woman who looks my way. I come home to you every night, but you still accuse me of cheating...we're just not good together. You like to party and you get angry when I tell you I'm tired."

Her face was marked by loathing. "Why shouldn't I have a good time? When you're home, all you do is work. It's always about your clients."

"You knew I was an attorney when we met." He paused a moment before asking, "If you find me so boring, why have you been pushing so hard for marriage?"

"All of my friends are getting married and it's not like I'm getting any younger, Austin. Any man would want me for a wife...anyone but you." Jasmine met his gaze. "But it's cool. You see, I know what you really want and it's the one thing you won't get. I'm gonna make sure of it."

He frowned. "What are you talking about?"

Jasmine shrugged, then closed her suitcase. "Doesn't matter."

Coming out of the musing, Austin looked down at the birth certificate in his hand as if seeing it for the first time.

He wasn't.

He had stared at it many times since procuring the copy from Jasmine's former best friend, Cheryl. They left Dallas, Texas, with Las Vegas in their sights.

Then one day Cheryl was back home. She requested a meeting with Austin, shocking him with the news that Jasmine was pregnant when they left town.

Austin could not believe she would just put the child up for adoption. He eyed the birth certificate once more. He was never listed as the father. In fact, the space was blank.

She had taken his son from him—the one thing that would hurt him most.

Chapter 1

"Aren't you going to dance with the bride?"

Austin's sister, Jadin, was standing before him.

His gaze slid to find her identical twin dancing with her new husband. Austin's mouth turned upward into a smile. "Maybe later. I don't think I've ever seen Jordin look so happy."

"She's just married the man of her dreams, big brother. She's completely over the moon."

A sea of people dressed in tuxes and bright dresses in summer colors roamed through the elegant space, admiring the paintings and photographs dotting the cream-colored walls. Surrounded by fourteen acres of live oak groves with serene views of the Ashley River, Austin's mind was elsewhere.

"You look distracted. Everything okay?"

"I'm fine," he responded. "Uh... Aunt Rochelle is trying to get your attention."

Jadin grimaced. "I guess I'd better see what she wants. That woman is getting on my last nerve today. Ever since she broke her ankle, she acts like I'm her personal maid."

"You volunteered your services, remember?"

"Do me a favor. Next time I open my mouth, punch me in it."

Austin bit back his amusement as he watched his sister make her way across the room. He hadn't known their aunt long, given his mother's determination to keep him from that side of his family, but it was enough to know she could be very demanding.

His eyes traveled to the table where the wedding party was seated. There were a couple of bridesmaids engaged in conversation. One of the ladies was Dr. Sabrina Collins, whom everyone affectionately called Bree—the woman who had adopted his son when Jasmine had placed him up for adoption.

Austin's gaze locked on her. She looked up, meeting his gaze. When she smiled, he felt the weirdest sensation— a strange mixture of both calm and excitement churning through his bloodstream like a virus, quickly spreading until he could hardly breathe.

Austin gave himself a mental shake. He wasn't looking for a romantic liaison. He sought to get back what had been taken from him. He never had the luxury of a relationship with his father, due in part to his mother's bitterness over losing the only man she ever loved to another woman. Her actions forced him to watch on the sidelines as his father doted on his twin sisters, Jordin and Jadin. Austin vowed his child would not tread down that same painful path.

With the help of a private investigator, Austin had succeeded in locating the child in Charleston, South Carolina. He thought it a blessing and fate that his son lived in the same city as his father and siblings. Austin had been taking steps to build a relationship with his family. Locating his son here, too, was perfect.

However, he was not prepared to discover that the woman raising his son was also the best friend of his sister, Jordin. This could be a potential complication, but he was not going to let this stop him from petitioning the courts to reverse the adoption.

Austin walked out on the balcony to enjoy the June weather. It was bright and sunny, but the temperature was just right. He agreed with guests who'd commented that the day was perfect for the wedding celebration.

He stood out there enjoying the picturesque grounds before navigating back through the doors and sea of wedding guests toward the nearest drink station, where he ordered a rum and cola.

At the sound of laughter, Austin turned in time to watch as Jordin and Ethan cut slices of their wedding cake. His sister looked happy and very much in love.

He smiled.

"What are you doing over here by yourself?"

Austin glanced over at his father. "Getting one last drink."

Etienne surveyed his face. "You okay, son?"

His gaze traveled back to Bree. "I am." The truth was that he had missed the first two years of his son's life and it filled his heart with an unrelenting ache. His pain was a shadow that resided in the corners of his heart but never failed to appear morning, noon or night.

"How are you dealing with the idea of Jordin being married?"

Etienne shrugged. "Ethan's a good man and he'll make her happy—of that, I have no doubt...but I have to confess, I'm feeling a mite old right now. All of my children grown..." He turned to face Austin, giving him a faint smile that held a touch of sadness. "I hate missing out on so much of your life."

"It wasn't your fault."

"It doesn't lessen the pain."

Austin believed his father because he felt the same way where Emery was concerned.

The office was empty when Austin arrived Monday morning around seven. He'd been working at his family's Charleston firm for a year but wasn't normally the first to arrive. Today he wanted to get an early start. It helped him to keep busy.

Austin entered the break room and made a cup of coffee.

The office manager, a woman in her early forties, walked in and gasped. "Oh, goodness... I'm sorry, Austin. I didn't expect anyone to be here. I'm usually the first to arrive."

"I woke up at five and couldn't go back to sleep, so I decided to come in a little earlier," he explained. "No point in wasting the time doing nothing."

She nodded in agreement. "I have to tell you...your sister's wedding was beautiful. Oh, my goodness... Your family really knows how to throw a wedding."

"It was nice," he told the office manager. "I enjoyed meeting your husband, Gwen. It turns out that I went to high school with the son of one of his frat brothers."

She smiled. "He told me. This world isn't as big as we think."

Austin couldn't agree more.

They talked a few minutes more while she waited for her tea to brew.

"I'd never been to Lowndes Grove Plantation before Jordin's wedding," Gwen stated. "And that house...it was stunning."

Austin agreed. "Jordin told me that it was built around 1786. The owners did a great job with the restorations."

"I almost want to have another wedding. Just to hold it there."

He smiled, then checked his watch. "Time to start my workday. I'm covering for Jordin while she's on her honeymoon."

"You've been pulling a lot of long hours, Austin." Gwen picked up her cup of tea. "Work-life balance, okay?"

"I'll keep that in mind." Austin took his coffee and headed to his office.

As soon as he sat down, his focus shifted to the stack of documents on his desk.

It was almost eleven when he called one of the paralegals and asked, "Were you able to get the information we needed from the mother?"

"Yes, I emailed it to you a few minutes ago."

"Thanks," he said before hanging up the phone.

Right after lunch Austin reviewed a couple of Jordin's cases. He appreciated the fact that she was so organized with everything he needed right where he could find it.

The sound of a baby crying in the hallway caught his attention, and he felt a wretchedness he'd never known before.

A stab of guilt lay buried in his chest. Maybe if he'd handled things with Jasmine differently, he might have had a chance to be with his son.

From everything he'd been told about Dr. Bree, Austin believed her to be a good woman. According to Jordin, she was also a very good mother to Emery. He wanted what was best for his child. It was this desire that conflicted him.

Austin intended to be a part of his son's life, but he worried about the effect it would have on Emery. He was safe and secure with Bree. The little boy didn't know he had a father. How would he respond when Austin made his presence known?

Austin walked back to his desk and picked up a file. He had just returned to the office from the courthouse. It was after five, but he wasn't quite ready to call it quits for the day. He'd always driven himself hard, putting work ahead of pleasure.

He also wanted to make his father proud. Austin had a lot of respect for both his father and uncle. Etienne and Jacques DuGrandpre had the same passion for law as their father, and his father before him. It was no wonder he, Jordin and Jadin all became attorneys.

It was in their blood.

He worked another two hours before shutting down his computer.

Tonight, he was leaving work earlier than usual. It was 7:30 p.m. Austin wanted to spend some time at the gym before he went home.

Just as he did every time he was on his way out, Austin paused in front of the large, looming portrait of Marcelle DuGrandpre, his grandfather. Austin's heart swelled with pride. Despite all odds during a time of racial tension, his grandfather opened the doors of the DuGrandpre Law Firm in 1960. When he died, Austin's uncle and father took over, the legacy continuing with their children.

"I miss him."

He hadn't heard anyone enter the room. Austin glanced over his shoulder. "Jadin, I didn't know you were still here. I thought I was the only one working late."

"Unfortunately, I will be putting in some long hours all week," she responded.

Austin had grown close to his twin sisters, Jadin and

Jordin, since moving to Charleston a little over a year ago from Dallas.

"I met him once," Austin told his sister. "Granddad was in town for a conference or something. He came to the house."

Jadin smiled. "I'm not surprised. He was all about family."

"I remember thinking that I was in trouble." Pointing to the portrait, he added, "He had that same stern expression on his face. But then he smiled at me."

"People used to think he was mean, but he wasn't. He would do anything he could to help others. He even offered his services pro bono to those who couldn't afford to pay."

"He was a good man. I'm glad I had the chance to meet him." Austin escorted Jadin to her car, then strolled down the next row to where his SUV was parked.

He drove the short distance to Holbrooke Boot Camp Gym, which was owned by his brother-in-law, Ethan.

He needed a strenuous workout to expend some of his pent-up energy. He'd been on edge ever since locating his son. Austin gathered his bag and navigated inside.

After a two-hour intense training, Austin still found himself wound tight, his frustration banked, but not eliminated.

When he arrived home, he pulled up his contact list on his phone. He stared at the names for a solid ten minutes before shutting it down. Austin considered calling a young woman he'd spent time with in the past, but changed his mind. She'd made it clear on several occasions that she wanted more than he was willing to offer.

Austin liked her, but she reminded him of Jasmine and that was a path he wasn't willing to travel down again.

He wasn't looking for a serious relationship now—his

thoughts were consumed with his son. Austin's heart ached with the knowledge that he had a child who was just beyond his reach.

Chapter 2

Bree Collins exited through the doors of New Beginnings Preschool, heading to her car. She checked her watch. She had taken Monday off to wind down after Jordin's wedding. Since Jadin was currently working on a high-profile case, Bree volunteered to run the necessary errands for the wedding, returning rental items and finalizing payment.

Today she wanted to get to the office early enough to have her first two cups of coffee while reviewing notes before the arrival of her clients.

Her receptionist was on the phone when she arrived.

"Good morning, Casey," Bree greeted.

"Hey, beautiful."

She loved the woman's bubbly personality and genuine demeanor. Her patients adored Casey.

"How was the wedding?" the receptionist asked.

"It was very romantic and beautiful," Bree responded. "I don't think it could've been more perfect."

Casey's infectious grin always set the tone for the day. "I know Jordin looked stunning."

"She did," Bree confirmed with a smile. "Speaking of weddings, have you and Eric set a date yet?"

Casey nodded. "We're getting married in October. On the tenth."

"That's wonderful."

"Now that we've picked our wedding day, the engagement feels more real to me." Casey handed her a stack of files. "You're booked all morning and two appointments after lunch."

"Light day…"

"Don't worry, you have a full day tomorrow."

Bree strolled into her office. Her eyes landed on the photograph of her son that sat on her desk. Her heart sang with delight whenever she thought about Emery.

When she lost her husband, Caleb, just before their second wedding anniversary, Bree wasn't sure she would ever recover. As a psychologist, she worked with others who were dealing with grief, but when it came to her own… Bree found herself in a bad state of mind.

It wasn't until she decided to adopt that she found hope again. When she met Emery, it was love at first sight. The moment she laid eyes on him—Bree knew he was the child for her.

Bree picked up Emery and headed home. She was thrilled to see her little boy and looked forward to spending some quality time with him after dinner. He was a very happy and secure soon-to-be three-year-old.

"Mommy, I wanna 'nana."

"Don't you want to eat dinner, sweetie?" she asked. "Mommy's making fried chicken and macaroni."

"Shick'en…mac'roni…yummy."

Bree laughed. "That's what I say. *Yummy.*"

As soon as they arrived home, she turned on the television for Emery, then went straight into the kitchen, where Bree washed her hands, then poured oil into a fryer. While it heated, she seasoned four chicken drumsticks and boiled water for the macaroni.

She placed the chicken in the fryer and the cheese and macaroni in the oven, put a load of Emery's clothes in the laundry and then returned to the kitchen. She washed her hands and checked on the food. Bree enjoyed being a mother. She considered it her one true purpose in life.

For a moment, she allowed herself to think about her late husband. He had been her best friend and she missed him. Enough time had passed since Caleb's death for Bree to consider dating.

Although she had gone on a few dates, she had not met a man who could hold her interest for one reason or another.

After dinner Bree cleared the table and filled the sink with hot water.

She was down to washing the skillet when the telephone rang.

A telemarketer.

Her mouth thinned with displeasure.

Bree put another load of clothes in the washing machine before giving Emery a bath.

She was glad that he went down easily. She hadn't finished the story before the little boy was sound asleep.

"My little man...you're so tired." Bree kissed his cheek. "Sleep well."

She tiptoed out the room.

Bree folded the rest of the laundry and carried it to her bedroom. She watched television as she put the clothing away.

After a quick shower, she got into bed with her laptop.

A friend of her emailed copies of the photographs she'd taken at Jordin's wedding. An easy smile curved her mouth as she scanned through them. She was truly happy for her friend. Ethan seemed to be a wonderful person and it was obvious that they were very much in love. Bree prayed they would have a long life together.

Her eyes landed on a photograph of Jordin's brother.

"You're a cutie, Austin DuGrandpre," she whispered. They hadn't been formally introduced, but she knew who he was—Jordin and Jadin spoke of him often.

Bree continued to stare at the photograph.

He looked so handsome in the light gray suit he wore. Tall, lean and muscular, Austin wore a smile that lit his chestnut-colored eyes and accented the tiny scar over his left eyebrow.

I wonder if he's dating anyone?

She chuckled to herself. She couldn't seriously be thinking about Jordin's brother in this manner.

Bree turned off the computer. If she hadn't, she'd be staring at Austin for the rest of the evening.

"*Mrs. Holbrooke*, it's nice to have you back," Austin greeted when Jordin strolled into his office a week later.

Her smile broadened. "I hear you've been holding down my clients for me. Thanks."

"I didn't have to do much."

Jordin sat down in one of the chairs facing him. "How are things with you?"

"I'm fine. Why?"

"We didn't get to finish our conversation about Bree and Emery."

"It was your wedding day—not the right time or place but nothing's changed," Austin responded, girding himself with resolve. "I want my son."

"I understand completely," Jordin said. "I would feel the same way if I were in your shoes. This is just such a complicated situation. I had no idea that Emery was your child. I celebrated with Bree when the adoption was finalized."

"I didn't know I was a father." He paused a moment before asking, "But you still think that I should wait?"

"For now," she responded. "I know Bree and you have nothing to worry about, Austin. She's a wonderful mother to Emery. She adores that little boy."

"He's *my* son. I never gave permission for him to be adopted."

"Unfortunately, courts have held that fathers unaware of their children may not later object to the children's adoption, particularly when the father's lack of knowledge was his own fault."

"I will argue that my lack of knowledge was due to dishonesty. Jasmine deliberately kept me in the dark about her pregnancy. She wanted to hurt me—I'm sure that's why she never told me that she was pregnant. Jasmine put Emery up for adoption because her boyfriend didn't want to raise another man's child."

"Don't take this the wrong way, but what did you do to her?" Jordin asked. "Why would she be so cruel?"

"She's always been vindictive. It's one of the reasons why we didn't work out as a couple. She wasn't happy when I broke up with her."

"But not telling you about the baby—it's malicious."

Austin nodded.

"I know how badly you want to unite with your son, but I suggest that you take some time and get to know Bree first before you say anything."

"Why should I do that?"

"Bree is also an innocent party in all of this, Austin. She doesn't deserve to be punished for loving your son. There has to be a way for you two to work this out."

He hadn't once considered Bree's feelings in this situation. Austin was simply focused on bringing his son home where he belonged, but his sister was right. Bree hadn't done anything wrong.

"Austin, I watched more than once as Bree suffered through bouts of endometriosis. She was in agony to the point it was crippling. I've never felt so helpless as to witness her pain and be unable to help her in some way. Finding out that she wouldn't be able to have children only made that pain worse. She once told me that she was born to be a mother and I believe her. If it's not handled carefully, losing Emery might just take all of the life out of her."

"Jordin, can you introduce us?" he asked. "Getting to know her might make this a little easier for everybody concerned."

She nodded. "Sure. Ethan and I were thinking about hosting a dinner party on Saturday. I'll invite her."

"Thanks so much, sis."

"I know you can't really see it right now, but I know that there's a way for you and Bree to come up with the perfect solution—one that will work for both of you."

"I don't intend to snatch Emery out of her arms, Jordin. I just want to be in his life. He's mine and I want to raise him. I'll be fair to Bree. I promise."

"He means the world to her."

"I haven't met him yet, but he already owns my heart, sis."

She nodded in understanding.

"How did she come to adopt him in Las Vegas?"

"Bree lived there for three years. Her husband was a musician and played for a couple of performers at Bally's. He died a year later…killed in a car accident. I think adopting Emery helped Bree heal through that horrible period in her life. When the adoption was final, she moved here to Charleston."

"Is she from this area?"

Jordin shook her head. "No, she's actually from Georgia. She was my college roommate and we clicked right from the beginning. She's been my best friend ever since."

She rose to her feet. "I'd better get to my office and return phone calls. I'm sure I have a stack of messages."

"You shouldn't," Austin said. "I talked to everybody who had called you up until yesterday."

"Thanks again, big brother." She paused in the doorway and said, "Oh, Austin... *I's married now.*"

He laughed. "That you are. One day I'll take that leap—don't know when, though."

"As soon as you find the right woman."

Austin thought about his sister's words. He'd once thought Jasmine was the right woman for him. She was anything but the right one. There was a time when he was crazy in love with her, but then Jasmine began taking him for granted. She used his love to manipulate him into doing whatever she wanted. When he finally came to his senses, the arguments started.

They tried to make it work for three years. Austin had no regrets when he broke up with Jasmine. He had thought long and hard and decided to do what was best for him.

But Jasmine had gotten back at him in the most hurtful way possible.

Austin didn't know if he would ever be able to forgive Jasmine for keeping his child away from him.

Nausea rolled through Bree, tightening her stomach and making her mouth water. She gripped the door frame. Any second now she was going to either throw up or wind up on the floor, doubled up in pain.

She hated being in such pain from her endometriosis, but was thankful that it wasn't as bad as it had been in the past. Bree sank down to the floor of the bathroom, the coolness of the ceramic tile against her skin bringing a measure of relief to her.

Her stomach rolled again as the spasms weakened her. One hand pressed to her mouth, Bree crawled over to the toilet.

Bracing her hands on her knees, her stomach released its contents.

For a long moment Bree remained where she was, weak and trembling, a sour taste in her mouth.

Finally, she pulled herself up, washed her face and brushed her teeth.

An hour later, Bree felt much better and was on her way to the office. It was Friday and she was looking forward to a weekend of fun and relaxation.

Jordin and Ethan were hosting their first dinner party tomorrow night. Bree wondered briefly who else would be in attendance. It didn't matter really. She was grateful to sit and have some adult interaction for an evening. It would be the perfect ending to a busy week.

Chapter 3

Austin arrived at Ethan and Jordin's home fifteen minutes early. He was surprised to find that Bree had already arrived. She was standing at the wrought iron railing on the second-floor balcony, facing Jordin as they talked.

He stared at Bree, looking her over. The deepening sunlight framed her figure, outlining her curves. She was beautiful in a simple, natural way. Austin was shocked to feel desire streaking through him like a current.

Jordin saw him and waved. "C'mon in. The front door is open."

Austin entered the house and was met by Ethan. "Hey…" he greeted. "Your wife told me to just walk in."

"No problem. Good to see you, man."

He heard footsteps behind him and turned to see Jordin descend the stairs followed by Bree.

"Austin, I want you to meet my best friend," she said. "Actually, she's more like a sister to me. Bree, this is my brother, Austin."

He was rendered speechless for a moment by her beauty. Austin swallowed hard, struggling to recover his voice. "It's a pleasure to meet you," he said finally.

His eyes darted to hers and locked.

He cleared his throat softly.

She met the smile and the hand that was offered. "It's a pleasure meeting you, as well. I've heard a lot about you."

Austin lost himself momentarily in their chocolate depths. His gaze fell to the creamy expanse of her neck. She was dressed to perfection in a teal-colored, sleeveless silk dress. Bree was tall and slender, but with an athletic build. She wore her shoulder-length hair in soft curls around her heart-shaped face. Her flawless skin was the color of a new penny.

"Dinner will be ready in a couple of minutes," Jordin announced. "We're still waiting on a few people to arrive."

"Would either of you like a glass of wine?" Ethan offered.

"I'm fine," Bree responded.

"Austin?"

"I'll take a glass."

Austin could feel Bree's eyes studying him. He met her gaze, forcing her to look away. He smiled to himself.

The front door opened.

"Hey, family," Ryker said with a grin. "Look at this… the newlyweds are hosting their first dinner party."

His wife, Garland, gave him a playful pinch. "Leave them alone."

There was something in the wistful turn of Bree's lips that made Austin sense the pain beneath the surface, and he longed to make it better. She had lost her husband in a tragic way and he could only imagine that while she was truly happy for Jordin—grief still resided in her heart.

Jadin arrived with a date a few minutes later, whom she introduced as Michael.

Austin leaned over and said to Bree in a low voice, "I guess we should've brought a plus one."

"I think you're right."

"Well, will you be my plus one for the evening?"

She turned, easing into a smile. "Sure."

Austin glanced up and saw Jordin standing in the doorway. She gave him a quick thumbs-up, then announced, "Dinner is ready."

He and Bree were seated beside one another.

"How do you like living in Charleston?" Bree inquired as she used her fork to slide the fettuccine noodles around her plate.

Austin smiled faintly, laid his napkin across his lap and, picking up his knife and fork, sliced into a strip of grilled chicken. "I'm enjoying it. I've always liked this area."

He took a bite of his food. The delicate Alfredo sauce and chicken were cooked to perfection.

"Jordin, did you cook this?"

Ethan chuckled and was awarded a sharp glance from her. "Just so you know, I *can* cook. I will confess that I called Aubrie for help with ingredients and such."

"It's delicious," Ethan said.

Everyone agreed.

"Does Aubrie ever hang out with the family?" Austin asked. "I think I've seen her maybe three times since I moved here. I'd like to get to know her better, especially since she's my first cousin."

"My sister spends a lot of her time in New Orleans," Ryker announced. "She goes there to spend time with the chef who mentored her in culinary school. Each time she comes back with new entrées for her restaurant."

Bree took a sip of her iced tea. "She must really enjoy her work."

"I'm not so sure this is just about her work," Jordin stated. "I think there's another reason why she spends so much time there."

Jadin agreed. "Aubrie isn't talking, but I suspect she's seeing someone."

"She was always one to keep secrets," Ryker said. "My parents keep hoping she'll come to her senses and join the firm, but it's not going to happen."

"How's Aunt Rochelle doing?" Jordin inquired.

"She hates being on crutches, having a cast on and not being able to drive. Mom's driving my dad crazy. He threatened to come stay with us until she's back on her feet." Ryker wiped his mouth on his napkin. "I love my mom, but when she doesn't get her way..."

"When Aunt Rochelle isn't happy—nobody's happy," Jadin said.

They all agreed.

When they finished their meal, they gathered in the family room.

Austin couldn't tear his gaze away from Bree.

Members of his family wandered in and out of his line of vision, locking Bree and him together, but nothing could shatter the connection alive and sizzling between them.

She felt it, too.

He could see it in her eyes, in the firming of her luscious lips. Just as he could see that she was trying to make sense of what she was feeling.

Their gazes connected and held.

Bree was an incredibly beautiful woman. Ravishing didn't even come close to describing her.

Austin broke eye contact with her and stared down into his glass of wine. He bit back a satisfied smile. Good to know he wasn't the only one being twisted into knots. However, he couldn't help but wonder if this attraction he felt would complicate his plan to get his son.

Bree was powerless to stop staring into the most beautiful set of eyes she'd ever seen. They were a stunning chestnut brown with golden flecks throughout, large and thickly lashed. Austin DuGrandpre bore a strong resemblance to his father. They had the same honey-colored skin, a muscular build and both stood about six feet three inches.

Men shouldn't have eyes this pretty, she thought.

He wore a light blue dress shirt that fit snugly over wide shoulders, then tapered, tucked into slim-waist navy trousers.

Austin smiled, revealing two small dimples Bree hadn't noticed before. She tried to throttle the dizzying current racing through her. He radiated a vitality that drew Bree like a magnet. Whenever he laughed, his full-throated masculine sound sent strange waves through her stomach.

Girl, you need to focus.

It wasn't easy, though. Austin made Bree feel things she hadn't experienced in a long time. Not since Caleb.

At least I still have those feelings, she reasoned silently. For a while she worried that they had died with her husband.

"Jordin told me that you're a psychologist."

"I am," Bree confirmed.

"I think it's cool. I've always been fascinated with human behavior, especially when it comes to the criminal mind."

"Okay, you know I'm going to ask the *question*. Why do you defend criminals?"

He chuckled. "I've come to expect it. All criminal defense lawyers are asked this question. It's part of the criminal defense experience."

"I'd like to hear your response, as well," Garland said. "I don't think it's something I could ever do, especially if I knew my client was guilty."

"Innocence is not the chief driver for me," Austin stated. "You all may find this strange but I enjoy working with guilty people. I have an interest in the causes of human conduct. I search to find the humanity in the people I represent, no matter what they may have done. I started out practicing family law, but I didn't find it as fulfilling," Austin said. "Nobody knows this, but I once considered studying forensic psychology. I have a bachelor's degree in psychology."

Bree reached for her glass. "Really?"

He nodded. "I love law and psychology—pursuing law just seemed the natural way to go for me."

There was something in his manner that she found soothing. It was easy to talk to him. "That's because you're a DuGrandpre," Bree responded. "It's in your blood."

"I suppose so," Austin said with a smile.

She felt a lurch of excitement within her. "It seems we have something in common," Bree told him. "I briefly considered going into law, but decided that I loved psychology more."

"Do you have any regrets?"

She shook her head. "I know that I'm exactly where I should be."

"I feel the same way."

Bree felt there was some type of deeper significance to the visual interchange between them.

The thought struck a vibrant chord in her.

She contributed to the conversation going on among everyone, but found herself studying his profile.

Bree had to deliberately shut out any awareness of Austin just to focus on Jordin's words.

"What do you think about a girls' night next weekend?"

"That's fine," she responded.

Jadin agreed, then asked, "What about you, Garland? Can you join us?"

"She can," Ryker answered for her. "It'll do her some good to get away from the children."

Garland pointed to him and replied, "What my husband said…"

At the end of the evening, she bid everyone a good night. As she gathered her purse, Austin volunteered to walk her down to her car.

"Bree, travel safe," he told her.

She tingled as he said her name and a quiver surged through her veins. "You do the same."

Bree unlocked the door and got into her car. She was soon pulling out of the driveway and traveling toward the freeway.

It had been a long time since a man had struck her interest, filling Bree with a strange inner delight.

Two days later Bree walked out of Marbelle's Children's Boutique, juggling her tote and a couple of shopping bags in her hands as she neared her car.

"Hey, are you following me?"

She glanced over her shoulder, her steps slowing. "Austin…what are you doing on my side of town?" Her heart danced with eagerness over seeing him again.

"I have a client who lives over here. Hey, thank you for being my plus one the other night. Everyone was coupled up…it could've been a little awkward if you hadn't been so gracious."

"I didn't mind. I enjoyed talking to you," she responded. "You're a very interesting man."

He grinned. "Do you have some time for lunch?"

"Sure." Bree looped her purse over her shoulder while her insides jangled with eagerness. She felt the blood surge from her fingertips to her toes. "So, where are we off to,

Austin DuGrandpre?" She was thrilled that he wanted to continue their conversation.

"There's a little place around the corner."

She chuckled a little. "You use that line often?" she asked playfully, glancing at him.

Austin laughed, full-throated and sexy. "I don't believe I've ever used it before, as a matter of fact." He adjusted his long stride to her much shorter one.

"I wouldn't recommend using it again," she remarked with a chuckle. "The only thing around the corner is a bank."

He laughed. "I'm still learning my way around."

"There's a sandwich shop that's two blocks away. It's walkable."

"Perfect. Let me help you with your bags," he offered.

They walked past a pizza place in full lunch swing, the scents of robust sauce and spicy sausage filling the air.

Bree's stomach rumbled. If he heard, there were no outward signs of it.

"You in the mood for pizza?" Austin inquired.

"Not really." Although the pizza smelled great, at noon the place was usually overrun by high school kids, and Bree didn't want to get caught in the wave of teens.

In the middle of the next block, the sandwich shop was trendy and casual.

"Have you been here before?" she asked.

"No. How's the food?"

"Very good. I highly recommend the club sandwich. It's roasted turkey breast, smoked ham with bacon and avocado. The roasted garlic mayonnaise is made in-house and is delicious."

"You find a table and I'll order our food," Austin suggested.

Bree found one near a large window facing the street. She hadn't expected to see him quite so soon. They would've run into each other at some point, she knew. This was perfect as she had been thinking of him earlier.

Austin walked up with two trays laden with sandwiches, potato chips, pickles and drinks.

Bree blessed the food.

"Jordin tells me that you have a little boy." He bit into his sandwich.

"I do," she exclaimed with intense pleasure. "He's my whole world." If Austin hadn't mentioned it, she would've told him about Emery. It's one of the first things she usually told men who seemed interested in her. It helped to eliminate the ones who were simply looking for a good time.

"That's cool."

"Do you have any children?" Bree inquired as she studied his profile.

It took a moment for him to respond. She wasn't sure he'd heard her. Bree opened her mouth to repeat the question.

"No," Austin interjected. "But I'm looking forward to having a child one day." He wanted to bring up the subject of Emery, but didn't want to make her suspicious as to why he'd be so interested in her son, especially since they'd just met.

"I think being a parent is probably my best achievement. My late husband and I really wanted children." She took a sip of her drink. "He would've loved Emery."

"I'm sorry for your loss."

Bree smiled. "Thank you, Austin. There was a time when it was hard for me to think about Caleb, but it's gotten easier. We had a lot of good times together."

"I can't imagine going through something like that."

Austin took another sip of his water when she moistened the top of her lip with the tip of her tongue. "I know my family would rally around me," he said, shifting slightly in his chair.

"You're lucky in that respect. I have no family," Bree stated flatly. "I've had to deal with everything alone." Austin had no idea just how lucky he was to have supportive family members. Anyone she'd truly cared about in the world was gone except for Emery.

"You're not close to them?"

"I grew up in a drug-infested apartment in Atlanta for the first six years of my life. My mom died of a drug overdose, and I lived with my paternal grandmother. When she died a couple of years later, I was placed with a foster family. I don't have any other relatives—at least any that I know about."

"I had no idea," he uttered.

Bree gave a slight shrug. "There's no way you could've known. Besides, it wasn't that bad. I had good foster parents. We lived in a nice neighborhood in Atlanta, with a great school. I was on the basketball team and even earned several college scholarships." She wiped her mouth with a paper napkin, then said, "I think I turned out okay."

"I agree," Austin said with a smile.

Bree settled back in her chair. "So, tell me about you."

"Well, I grew up believing that my dad cared more for his twin daughters than he did me. Moving here and spending time with him, I found out that it wasn't the case and that I'd wasted a lot of time being angry with my father."

"Jordin adores you," she said. "Jadin, too."

"I have two incredible sisters."

"What made you choose law, Austin?" Bree asked. "Especially since you were angry with your father during that time?"

"I think it was a way for me to feel close to him. Maybe I wanted to make him proud."

"What's the story behind that scar above your eye?" she questioned.

"You noticed?" He grinned. She smiled back.

"When I was in the ninth grade, I got into a fight with a bully at school. He picked up a stick and hit me with it."

"Wow... I hope he got the worst of it."

"Oh, I left some scars," Austin stated. "When I saw that I was bleeding, I lost it. I was told that it took three people to get me off him."

"I had a fight in high school," Bree said. "It was with a jealous teammate. She got into some trouble in one of her classes, so she had to sit out a game. It was my chance to finally show the coach what I could do, so I took it and I got her spot." She sipped her tea. "The thing is I really needed to be noticed—it was the only way I could go to college. My foster parents were good to me, but they'd made it clear that with four kids—we needed to try to get as many scholarships as possible."

Austin took a sip of his drink. "My dad paid for my college education and trust me, I'm grateful. I've already started an education fund for my children."

"I thought you didn't have any," Bree interjected.

"It's never too early to start planning," he responded.

She smiled. "You're a very smart man, Austin. I have a college fund for my son, as well."

It pleased Austin to hear this. At least Emery had been placed with a responsible woman. "How did you end up in Vegas? Was it because of your husband?"

"After I graduated, I landed a great job there with a mental health center. My husband was a musician and found work right away—it just worked out. But when he died, I didn't want to stay in Nevada. Jordin had been urging me to move closer to her for years, and since she was the closest thing I had to family, I moved to Charleston and decided to open my own practice."

"When I was growing up, people didn't openly admit to seeing a psychologist. They didn't even talk about mental illness," Austin countered.

"In the African American community, there are still some people who consider mental illness to be a white person's disease," Bree stated. "It's terrible because statistics tell a different story. Twenty percent of blacks are more likely to experience some form of mental illness than Caucasians."

"I think it has to do with socioeconomic disparities from slavery to race-based exclusions when it comes to health care."

"It's true," Bree said. "People who live in poverty or have substance abuse problems are at higher risk for poor mental health."

Austin couldn't help admiring her intelligence and compassion.

They finished off their meal.

"I'm glad I ran into you," Austin told her. "I hate eating alone."

"Same here." She wrenched herself away from her ridiculous preoccupation with his arresting face.

"Bree, that's not exactly true," Austin confessed. "The truth is that I'd like to get to know you better. I enjoy your company."

His words pleased her. "I'd like to know more about you, as well."

They exchanged phone numbers.

Bree checked her watch. "I need to get back to my office. I have several appointments this afternoon."

He took her hand in his and kissed her on the cheek. "Until next time."

"Goodbye," she whispered, pulling her hand away from his grasp, his touch sending shivers through her.

Their steps were hurried once they exited the shop. She needed to get to her office and Bree was sure that Austin had to return to work, as well.

Many hours later she still couldn't escape the gentle look he'd given her as they parted ways.

That evening the phone rang as Bree came out of the bathroom, clad in flannel pajama bottoms and a T-shirt. She padded barefoot around the king-size bed to answer it.

"Hey, it's Austin."

She hadn't expected to hear from him so soon, but his call thrilled her. "What's up?"

"I wanted to tell you again that I had a great time with you. I'm glad we ran into each other."

Bree's heart was hammering foolishly. "Same here."

"Do you have some time to talk?"

"Yes," she responded. "Emery's sleeping, so we're good."

They made small talk for a few minutes before Austin said, "Bree, I have a confession to make. I'm very attracted to you and I'd like to take you out. That is if you're not involved with anyone." He gave a short laugh. "I guess I should've asked this first."

She couldn't deny the spark of excitement she felt at the prospect of dating him. "I'm single, Austin. As for spending time with you—I don't have a problem with it. You're not exactly what I'd call boring."

"I guess the next step is when and where. How about tomorrow night?"

"I need to check my calendar really quick," she said. "I have to attend a fund-raiser at my son's preschool. I'm not sure if its tomorrow or the next day." Bree quickly checked the calendar on her cell phone. "Okay, tomorrow I'm free."

"Can you get a babysitter lined up for your son or is this late notice?" Austin inquired.

"It's not a problem. I have someone who can pick him up from school. She watches him for me whenever I need her. She lives next door."

"That's great to hear." Austin didn't have a problem with her bringing Emery, but Jordin had forewarned him that he couldn't rush Bree where the child was concerned. She didn't bring her dates around Emery until she felt the time was right.

They spent the next sixty minutes on the phone talking.

Bree hung up to call her neighbor. "Hey, Miss Sara. How are you?"

"I'm fine, sugar. How's my li'l sweetie?"

"He's doing fine," she responded with a smile. "I'm calling to see if you can watch Emery for me tomorrow evening. I'm going on a date."

"It's about time you got out and found yourself a nice man. I been praying for you."

Bree laughed. "He seems pretty nice." Just thinking about Austin sent shivers of delight down her spine.

"Now, don't you worry about Emery. I'll pick him up from school and make him some spaghetti. We'll have ourselves a good time."

"Save me a plate of spaghetti, Miss Sara." She and Emery both loved pasta. "And thank you."

"It's my pleasure, Bree. You know it's no trouble at all."

She checked on Emery, then made her way to the master bedroom.

Inside she crossed the room toward the walk-in closet. Bree pulled out a black pantsuit to wear to work the next day. She didn't like waiting until the last minute to decide on an outfit. Her eyes landed on vibrant blue maxi dress hanging in the closet.

Bree took it and hung it on the door. *I'll wear this tomorrow night*. It was the perfect "first date" dress. Not too sexy, but showed enough skin to hold Austin's attention.

She was excited. This was the first date she'd had in probably six months. Bree hadn't been sitting down twiddling her thumbs, though. Emery and her work kept her very busy. However, if things went well with Austin; her schedule might open a bit more.

Bree had a good feeling about him. Jordin had always spoken highly of Austin and she could see why. He was charismatic, bringing an air of sincerity with it. It was refreshing to be able to talk to someone who understood her field of work and showed a genuine interest in it. Bree hadn't really put too much thought into it before, but some of the guys she'd dated in the past weren't comfortable with her because they felt that she was analyzing them.

A smile lingered on her lips. There was something different about Austin. If she wasn't careful, this man would own her heart.

Bree stifled a yawn. She was exhausted, but it was still too early for her to go to bed.

She thought she heard a sound and quickly made her way to her son's room.

He had changed positions, but was sound asleep.

She stood there, watching him, her heart swelling with pride. Bree sent up a silent prayer of thanks to God for sending her this beautiful little angel.

She padded barefoot to the bookcase in the family room where the photo albums were kept on the bottom shelf. She ignored the dust gathering. There hadn't been time for dusting because of her busy schedule. Bree pulled out a small blue album—Emery's baby book, taking it with her to the couch.

You were such a tiny little thing. Fragile and amazing.

From the moment Emery was placed in her arms, a fountain of love rose within her, stronger than any force she'd known. Bree traced her fingertip along the button shape of his cute little face, and gazed at those beautiful brown eyes staring up at the camera.

She drank in a last long look at Emery's innocent, sweet face, and the love within her strengthened, just as it did every time she saw her son.

The slam of the neighbors' car door cut through Bree's thoughts. She closed the album and slipped it back onto the shelf as the muted sound of voices outside shattered the peaceful silence of her home.

Chapter 4

Austin's hour-long phone conversation with Bree confirmed that he wasn't mistaken in the connection they'd made the moment they met. He had felt an immediate and total attraction. Austin looked forward to seeing her tomorrow evening and beyond.

He settled down in his favorite chair, his fingers dancing to the jazz melody playing on the iPad nearby. His heart beat with the pulse of the music.

The one good thing to come out of this situation with Jasmine was the little boy he had yet to meet. He believed that Bree was a good mother, which put him at ease. Just the short time they'd spent together, he could sense that she had a warm, loving spirit; she was intelligent and caring. There was also an undeniable magnetism building between them.

She's the type of woman I could see myself spending the rest of my life with.

The silent declaration surprised him, but it was the truth. He wasn't just attracted to her physically, he was also attracted to her mind.

A cloud of apprehension settled over him.

How would she react when he announced that he was Emery's biological father? Would it change anything between them?

Austin knew the day would come when he would have to tell Bree of his intentions. As much as he looked forward to building a relationship with Emery, he dreaded the thought that his love for his son might cause her some pain. He hoped that his relationship with Bree would be solid enough to handle the truth.

Notepad and pen in hand, Austin strode into the conference room ten minutes before the meeting was supposed to start and took a seat beside Jordin.

"I'm seeing Bree tonight," he announced in a low voice.

She stared, complete surprise on her face. "To do *what*?"

"Jordin, relax. We're having dinner together. You told me that I should get to know her—well, that's what I'm doing."

"I think it's the best approach," she responded. "But I don't want you leading her on, Austin. She doesn't deserve to be hurt."

"I have no intentions of misleading her, sis. Bree seems like a nice person and I can tell by the way she talks about Emery that she's a devoted mother."

"I can assure you that she loves that little boy with her entire being, Austin. He's happy and secure."

"I can't wait to meet him."

"You can't rush this," Jordin warned. "The goal is to get to know Bree and give her a chance to know you before you drop the baby bomb. I'm sure she's considered the possibility of Emery's biological parents looking for him one day, but I'm also sure that's not a scenario she thought could happen anytime soon. You're going to have to tell her the truth when you feel the time is right, but you need to give her a chance to see the type of man you are. The last thing you, Bree or Emery needs is an unnecessary court battle. I don't think that would be very good for any of you."

"Or you?" Austin challenged.

"Or me," Jordin conceded. "I pray she'll forgive me for keeping this from her. My only hope is that everything will work out for the best this way and she'll understand why I kept silent." She wiped her hands over her eyes. "Not to mention how the rest of the family is going to act when they learn the truth."

Their conversation came to a pause when Jadin entered the room. Austin had chosen to keep his secret just between him and Jordin.

Austin smiled at her. "Congratulations on your win in court yesterday."

"Thanks," Jadin responded. "I'm *so* glad that case is over. I'm thinking about taking next week off just to relax." She leaned back in her seat. "Lord knows I need it."

"You should do it," Jordin said. "I know how hard you've worked for the last six months preparing for trial."

Austin agreed.

"Sooo," Jadin began. "Did you make a little love connection the other night? I noticed you and Bree seemed to be in your own little world. You two talked the whole night."

He chuckled. "We had a nice conversation."

Amused, Jadin met his gaze. "I'd say it was a lot more than that, big brother."

"I'm not denying it. *I like her.*"

"That much is obvious," Jadin interjected. "So, when are you seeing her again?"

"I'm having dinner with her this evening."

Jadin clapped her hands. "Well done."

Austin turned in his chair to face her. "Your date… that's the Michael I've heard so much about? I didn't get a chance to talk to him much at Jordin's."

"That's because you were so into Bree," Jadin responded. "But yes, that's him. I intended to come alone, but he called to let me know he was in town, so I invited him to join me."

"How are things between you two?" Jordin inquired. She pushed away from the table, got up and strolled over to the coffee station.

"Good. He keeps telling me that he's committed to making our relationship work."

Etienne strolled into the room, followed by his brother Jacques.

Other members of the legal team arrived minutes later.

Austin picked up his pen as one of the secretaries passed out copies of the agenda. He hoped this meeting was not one that lasted more than a couple of hours. He wanted to leave the office no later than five o'clock. They had dinner reservations at High Cotton for six thirty, then would return to his place for coffee and dessert.

A smile formed on his lips as an image of Bree entered his mind. Austin made a mental note to ask Jordin about her favorite dessert—he figured it would be a nice way to end the evening.

Austin left the office fifteen minutes later than he'd planned.

He drove out of the Ashley Bakery parking lot, merging into the traffic. Austin pulled up to a stop light, bobbing his head to the song playing as he waited patiently for the light to change.

Austin felt the tiny hairs on the back of his neck stand up.

He glanced out the window, his eyes landing on a gorgeous woman in the car beside him. Austin gave a slight nod in greeting.

She flashed him a sexy grin and winked.

The light changed and Austin was on his way, harboring no regret for not getting her name and number. He didn't care for women who were so flirtatious. He'd had enough of that with Jasmine.

Austin pulled into an underground parking garage ten minutes later.

He got out of the car, grabbed the cake and his briefcase. He walked with purpose through the lobby and into a waiting elevator.

Austin prepped his condo, making sure it was guest ready, then hopped into the shower.

He was dressed and ready by six just in case Bree arrived earlier than expected. She struck him as a woman who was always early to avoid being late. The thought prompted a self-conscious smile.

Austin was about to retrieve a bottle of water from the refrigerator when the doorbell rang. He'd called down to the doorman and told him to send Bree up when she arrived. He stole a quick peek to his watch.

Ten after six.

Smiling, he opened the door.

The vision standing before him left him momentarily speechless.

Bree wore her hair in a mass of loose curls that fell to her shoulders. The wrap dress reached to the floor, giving him a peek of her shapely legs as she walked. He couldn't resist admiring her slender frame and soft curves. She made his temperature rise more than a little.

He wondered if she knew just how sexy she looked.

"I'm early, I know," she said. "I don't like being late anywhere."

Austin bit back his smile. "It's fine. I'm the same way." They had more in common than he would've imagined. Add this to his attraction to her...his feelings for Bree were confused and confusing. He didn't know how to describe them and was too afraid to analyze them.

Bree had opted to meet him at his place since he lived in the downtown area on Concord Street. She surveyed the contemporarily furnished condo Austin called home. She loved the acacia hardwood floors, the double balconies and the gorgeous view of the city. "You have a very nice place."

"Thank you." Austin's eyes bounced around the room. "It needs a woman's touch, though, and probably more furniture."

"I think the way it is actually fits your personality. You don't strike me as a man who likes a lot of stuff in your space. I would say that you're a minimalist. You look put together always, but you're not one to fuss over your looks. You're probably more comfortable in what you have on right now than in a suit and tie or a tuxedo."

Austin had dressed down for the evening. Long, muscled legs filled out faded jeans, and he wore a plain black T-shirt that accentuated the broadness of his torso.

"You're right," he said. "I'm impressed."

Austin grabbed his keys and they headed down to his SUV.

Ten minutes later, they were seated at a table with a scenic view of the street.

Austin had suggested High Cotton Restaurant. She had eaten there a few times, and the food was always excellent. It was her absolute favorite eatery. Bree found the atmosphere at High Cotton relaxing and the food tantalizing. Their first date was off to a great start.

"Why did you choose this place for dinner?" she asked, her gaze fixed on his handsome face.

"It's a favorite of mine," he responded. "Have you been here before?"

She grinned. "Another thing we have in common. I *love* this restaurant."

"I'm glad. I was a little reluctant to try someplace new since this is our first date. I knew what to expect here."

He ordered wine.

All around them, couples sat at tables, leaning toward each other, smiling, laughing, talking. Waitresses moved through the room serving up orders of bar food and drinks. The clink of glassware and the ripples of conversation became a white noise that hummed in the background.

Bree stared into Austin's chestnut-brown eyes and fought to hold on to the control and willpower she had developed over the past few years.

It wasn't easy.

When the waitress returned, she took their food order. Bree ordered the jumbo crab cakes while Austin chose shrimp and grits.

"Tell me more about this wonderful son of yours."

Bree was touched that Austin seemed interested in Emery. "Well, he's almost three and keeps me very busy. I'm not complaining, though. My son brings me so much joy. It's hard to put into words what it means to be a mother."

"It's clear to me that you really enjoy it."

"I've always wanted to be a mother. A short time after

Caleb and I married, I found out that my chances of having a child naturally were very slim. We decided to adopt, but then he passed away. When I felt ready emotionally, that's when I moved forward and Emery came into my life." She looked away. "That's probably more than you wanted to know on a first date."

"No, I admire you for being so transparent."

"I love my son so much—it doesn't matter that he didn't come from my body."

"He's a very lucky little boy."

Bree's eyes grew bright with unshed tears. "I'm the lucky one, Austin. I'm sure every mother says this, but I know this to be true—Emery is a very special child. He loves in such a pure way. When he smiles at me or gives me a kiss… I can't describe the feeling I get." She took a sip of her wine. "I'm sorry for going on like that."

"No need to apologize, Bree. I asked about Emery." He paused a moment before saying, "I'm sure you're just dying to show me a picture of him."

"I have many," she responded. "Would you like to see them?"

Austin nodded.

Bree pulled up some photos on her cell phone and handed it to him.

"He's a handsome little boy."

"Thank you."

She watched as Austin stared at the photos. Bree had never met a man who was so taken with Emery, especially since they hadn't even met.

Their food arrived.

"How's the crab cakes?" Austin asked.

"Delicious as always." She leaned forward and said in a low voice, "I'm trying not to devour them. Don't want to ruin your impression of me after one date."

He chuckled. "I don't think that's possible."

Bree regarded him with amusement. "I don't know if Jordin told you anything about me, but what you see is what you get."

"I like that," he responded. "I prefer to be around someone who isn't afraid to be herself."

She wiped her mouth on her napkin. "It's the only way I know how to be."

He broke into a grin. "It's nice to meet another well-rounded individual."

Laughter rang out between them.

After dinner, they returned to his condo.

Austin had teased over dinner that he had a surprise for her. Bree couldn't imagine what it could be, and could hardly contain her excitement.

Before taking a seat in the living room, she caught glimpses into other rooms. A formal dining room and an office with floor-to-ceiling bookshelves.

In the room where she sat, a wall beyond the fireplace was covered with bookshelves filled with books. Bree settled back in the chair. It was a very nice house, shabby and comfortable, clean but not too neat. All it lacked was the warmth of a woman's touch...

"I'll be right back," Austin said before disappearing into the kitchen.

Moments later he returned with two slices of banana chocolate chip cake on plates. "Is this from Ashley Bakery?"

Nodding, he smiled. "Now, I have to confess that I asked Jordin about your favorite dessert, but the restaurant was my idea."

"This is the perfect way to end the night," she murmured. "Thank you, Austin."

He seemed to be peering at her intently.

"What is it?"

"You are so beautiful."

Austin looked at her as if he were trying to photograph her with his eyes.

"You should try the cake," Bree said. "It's really delicious. It's also Emery's favorite."

She shifted her focus from his face to her plate. Her body ached for his touch and she didn't want to get too caught up in her own emotions. What she felt—her feelings for him had nothing to do with reason.

This is a first date. Slow down, girl.

Austin sampled the dessert. "This is really good. I've always been a carrot cake lover, but this is *good.*"

"A new convert…yeah!"

They laughed.

"I've already packaged up half of the cake for you to take home with you."

"You've just made my baby a very happy little boy. He was asking for some earlier. I'd promised him that we'd pick up a cake this weekend."

Bree was impressed with Austin's unselfish actions. He hadn't known her long, but he was interested in her likes and dislikes. He was considerate in including her son, which scored him major points with her.

Austin brought the half of the cake he'd packaged up for her. "Here you go."

Bree didn't want to keep her babysitter up too late as it was a weeknight and she usually went to bed early. She rose to her feet. "Tonight was amazing," she said. "Thank you for everything."

He moved closer, challenging Bree to deliberately shut out any awareness of him.

"I have another confession to make."

Looking up at him, she asked, "What is it?"

Bree was lifted in the cradle of Austin's arms. "There's something I've wanted to do all evening," he said, his voice just above a husky whisper.

Her body tingled when he touched her.

His lips were warm and soft, and she let go of any misgivings and kissed him back, her heart leaping. Austin was gentle and devastating as his mouth slid from hers and dropped fleeting kisses on her cheeks and her eyes.

When they parted, Bree's lips still burned from the delicious sensation of his kiss.

He walked her down to her car.

"Call or text me when you get home," Austin told her. "I want to know that you made it home safely."

"I will."

He planted another kiss on her lips.

Bree sang along with the radio all the way home.

When she arrived, a full-figured woman wearing a T-shirt and jeans came down the stairs.

"I can tell you had a good time. You practically floating right now."

Bree smiled despite herself. "Miss Sara, what are you talking about?"

"What's that in your hand?"

"He surprised me with a banana chocolate chip cake for dessert," Bree announced. "He gave me half to bring home."

"High Cotton for dinner and then your favorite cake... now that's my kinda man. I'm liking this boy already."

Bree held up her phone. "I need to text him to let him know I'm home safe."

"I made some tea," Sara announced. "Want a cup?"

She handed her neighbor the cake. "Sure. Feel free to have some cake. It's from Ashley Bakery."

"Girl, you talking my language. I'ma have a tiny slice of that cake with my tea and then I'ma go home and get in the bed."

Bree sent a quick text to Austin, then sat and talked with her neighbor while they drank tea.

When Sara left for her place, she made sure all the doors were locked, turned on the security alarm and checked on Emery. He was sound asleep, clutching a Spider-Man toy. He always took a superhero to bed with him.

She ran her fingers softly through his curls, then kissed him on the cheek.

Bree stifled a yawn as she navigated to her bedroom, where she turned on the TV and prepared a bath.

Stepping out of the bubbles fifteen minutes later, she wrapped a thick blue towel around herself and stared in the mirror. Austin's kiss still lingered on her lips. Bree closed her eyes, reliving the way he smelled and the feel of his muscles. His touch was imprinted in the places he'd touched her. It amazed her that a good-night kiss could awaken her in areas that had lain dormant since Caleb's death.

She'd gone on dates in the past, but none lasted more than a couple of months at best. Bree's focus stayed on her son and building her client base. She wanted to remarry, and had no doubt that she would when the right man came along. After an entertaining evening with Austin, she felt that he had a lot of potential in terms of a relationship.

The sound of the television in the bedroom infiltrated her musings. One of those reality shows was on. *Give me a good book any day*, she thought.

Stifling a yawn, she slipped on a nightgown, then padded into a bedroom decorated with a soothing color scheme of purple and silver-gray with black accents.

Bree was more than ready to dive into the four-poster

bed. Her day had been a long one, but so worth it, she decided.

Her summer was off to a great start.

Chapter 5

He tossed an ink pen on his desk before leaning back in his chair. For the umpteenth time that day Austin was reminded of the kiss he'd shared with Bree the previous night. A kiss he had taken before she'd been aware he was about to do so. He sucked in a sharp breath as more memories swept through his mind. Never had a woman's mouth tasted so delectable, so irresistibly sweet. He'd also learned more about his little boy. Unshed tears pricked Austin's eyes when Bree had shown him the photographs of Emery.

His arms held the memory of how she felt in them. She was warm, comforting and solid. This was the type of woman he wanted in his life. Someone he could lean on and not fall. And there would come a time when he would need her strength—Austin couldn't explain how, but he knew it to be true.

The more Austin pondered the thought, he realized that it most likely came from a conversation with his mother. Irene used to always tell him that he needed a life partner who would stand strong when he couldn't. One who would not see it as weakness.

Jasmine had called him weak once. She didn't think he

could stand up to his mother. Austin could never get her to understand that he alone made the decision to break up with her—it had nothing to do with Irene. Truth was that he never would've been with Jasmine had he listened to his mother.

Austin knew that Irene would approve of Bree. She was the type of woman his mother always said he deserved.

He felt a thread of guilt snake down his spine. Irene didn't know she was a grandmother. For that matter, Etienne knew nothing about Emery, either. Everyone was in the dark and this secret was beginning to weigh heavily on him.

An hour later Austin had finished an important document his cousin Ryker needed. He had one more file to read, which wouldn't take long. Then, before leaving for the day, he would call Bree to check in. She would be spending the evening with Jordin, Jadin and Garland—it was their girls' night out.

Bree plopped down on the sofa in her living room after a long day at work. She needed to take some downtime before heading over to Jordin's house. She was really looking forward to a night of food, drinks and merriment.

She had already stopped in at Sara's house to check on Emery. He was too busy with his new picture book to pay much attention to her.

An hour later Bree changed into a pair of jeans and a tank top. She grabbed her keys and drove to Jordin's house. She pulled in behind Garland's car and parked.

"Where's Ethan?" Bree asked. "You didn't kick him out of the house for us, did you?"

"He's spending time with his mother," Jordin responded. "They went to dinner and then they're going to see a movie. They do this twice a month."

Bree smiled. "That's really sweet. He's come a long way."

"I have you to thank for your part in this. Talking to you helped Ethan tremendously." Jordin gestured for Bree to join her. "Here…try this. It's a new recipe."

"This chocolate sauce is delicious," she said. "Are you going to put this on top of the bread pudding?"

"Yes, that was the idea. What do you think?"

"I think it's yummy as Emery would say."

Jordin chuckled.

"Where's Jadin?" Bree asked as she poured three glasses of wine. "I thought she was coming by." She handed one to Garland and one to Jordin.

"Michael's in town. He surprised her earlier today at the office."

Shaking her head, Garland uttered, "I don't know why she won't marry that man. It's obvious that she loves him."

Jordin sipped her wine. "She's sold on our grandfather's legacy of lawyers. Michael's uncle holds a chain of luxury hotels and he was thrilled for the opportunity to be the general manager for the newest one."

Bree sat her glass down on the counter. "Are you talking about the Alexander-DePaul hotels?"

"Yes." Jordin peeked into the oven to check on the bread pudding. "Malcolm Alexander is his uncle."

Arms folded across her chest, Bree leaned back against the granite countertop. "I read the story of how Robert DePaul left everything to the son nobody knew he had. I assumed he was the only child."

"Malcolm's stepbrother is Michael's father."

"How do you think he feels about the long-distance relationship?" Garland questioned.

"Jadin's the one struggling with it," Jordin stated. "She's

tried to end it a couple of times, but Michael's not going to give up on them."

"She'd better hold on to that man," Bree said. "Trust me, being single is not always fun."

"I agree," Jordin responded. "I'm really loving marriage."

"I want someone to knock me off my feet like Caleb did. I'm so ready to be married, pampered and placed on a pedestal by a man who adores me."

"Are you saying that Austin hasn't done that for you?"

She met Jordin's smile with one of her own. "He and I have a good time together. He's a lot more settled, which works for me as the older I become. But I have to admit that I'm kind of falling for him."

Bree stirred the chocolate sauce while Jordin took the bread pudding out of the oven and set it on top of a cooling rack.

"I'm pretty sure my brother feels the same way about you, too."

"I haven't introduced him to Emery yet," Bree announced.

"What are you waiting on?"

"I just feel that it's still a bit too soon," she explained. "I want to wait a bit more to see where the relationship is heading before I bring my son into it."

Bree stirred the sauce once more. "Girl, just smelling this chocolate, I can already feel myself putting on pounds. You know that's the last thing I need right now."

Garland nodded in agreement. "It does smell good."

"Bree, you look great," Jordin told her. "The last thing you need to worry about is weight gain."

"Don't get me wrong, I'm happy with the way I look," she quickly explained. "I just don't want to have to buy new clothes."

Jordin chuckled. "Girl, all I need is an excuse to shop."

"I know. I used to hate going to the mall with you—we'd be there all day long."

"That's why I always treat you to a power breakfast so that we could build up your strength."

Laughing, Bree shook her head. "Since we're on the topic of shopping, what did you buy yesterday? You were leaving some store when I called you."

"That's right," Jordin murmured. "Let's go to my bedroom and get them."

She returned moments later with a shopping bag.

"Aren't these adorable?" Jordin asked, holding up two pink and lavender dresses with matching hats.

"Precious..." Bree murmured.

"Did you get those for the girls?" Garland asked, referring to her young daughters.

Jordin nodded. "When I saw them, I just couldn't resist."

"Kai and Amya are going to love them." Garland fingered one of the dresses. "They're gorgeous."

"And I got this for little R.J. I bought this outfit because the cap looks like the one Ryker wears."

Garland grinned. "He's going to look just like his daddy."

Jordin pulled another outfit out of the bag. "I didn't forget my sweet Emery."

Bree took the gray linen suit from her. "This is so cute. It's adorable." She looked at her friend. "You're spoiling these kids."

"Yes, you are," Garland said. "The girls already know that they can get whatever they want from you."

"They're worth it," Jordin responded. "They're my babies."

She pulled a plate of sandwiches out of the refrigerator, placing them on the counter.

"Ethan and I are planning a cruise," Jordin announced, lounging against the door frame. "Do y'all think you'd be interested in coming with us?"

"I've never been on one," Bree said. "I don't know..."

"Please come on the cruise so that I'll have somebody to hang out with when Ethan's playing basketball or golf or whatever guy stuff he can get into."

"What about Austin? Have you invited him?" Bree asked. "I don't want to be a third wheel if I decide to come."

"I plan on asking him, but wanted to ask you first before I said anything to him."

"I have to think about this for a moment," Bree said.

"Is this going to be a couple's vacation or a family one?" Garland inquired, wedging herself into the seat next to her.

"It's up to you all," Jordin responded. "It'll work either way for me and Ethan."

"Give me all the information and I'll let you know for sure."

Jordin opened the refrigerator and pulled out a couple of steaks. "We're planning for next summer, so we have some time."

Garland munched on some chips. "What are you doing?"

"Taking the steaks out for dinner tomorrow."

Bree broke into a grin. "Aren't you quite the home-maker."

Jordin nodded. "Hey, I need to feed my husband or some other woman will be more than happy to do it for me."

She nodded in agreement. "I love seeing you so happy."

Jordin met her gaze. "I'm over the moon, Bree. I love

being married and I can't wait to be a mother. I'm so ready for a family."

"You're going to be a great mother."

Jordin's expression grew somber. "How have you been feeling lately?"

"Some months are much better than others," Bree said.

Garland inquired, "Are the treatments helping?"

"Not as much as I'd like. The pain can be overbearing at times."

"Bree, I'm so sorry you have to suffer like that," Jordin stated. "Endometriosis is nothing to play with."

"It's a horrible disease," she responded. "But I've learned to live with it."

Bree sampled the white chocolate bread pudding. *"You did that..."*

Jordin beamed with pride. "You really think so?"

"Yes. This is *soo* good."

Garland agreed.

Bree rose in one fluid motion. "I'm just going to have a tiny bit more."

"Girl, dig in," Jordin told her. "You're in the gym three days a week. You can afford to treat yourself."

"Chocolate *is* a girl's best friend," Garland interjected. "Bree, how do you like dating a DuGrandpre?"

"It's not something I ever thought I'd be doing," she said. "But that's because Ryker was the only male I knew and he was married."

"Did you ever meet Angela?" Garland asked, referring to Ryker's first wife, who died in childbirth.

"I did," Bree replied. "Shortly after she and Ryker got married. She was really nice to me."

"Sometimes I wonder if he's thinking of her when he looks at Amya," Garland confessed. "She looks more and more like Angela the older she gets. It's fine if he does...

I just want Ryker to feel comfortable talking about her. I won't feel threatened in any way. Besides, Amya will have questions one day."

"Maybe you should bring her up," Bree suggested. "This will open up an opportunity for Ryker to talk about Angela. Let him know that it doesn't bother you if he wants to talk about their life together."

Jordin agreed. "I love a good love story. The one you're writing with Ryker is inspiring."

"Yes, it is," Bree murmured. "The two of you give me hope."

Garland took a sip of her wine. "From where I'm sitting, it looks like you're writing your own love story with Austin."

She broke into a grin. "Well, I have to admit that we have a lot of sexual tension but we haven't gotten to the chapter where we fall into bed and make wild, passionate love."

"Do you think it's heading in that direction?" Jordin asked. "It's still pretty early in your relationship."

"I don't know, but it's not something I'm dwelling on. You know me...my focus is on being a mother to Emery. I'm not thirsty for a man. It's just nice to have someone like Austin to spend time with. *He is sexy, though.*"

Jordin screwed up her face. "Okay, don't need to hear that..."

They laughed.

"Seriously, though, take your time with Austin," Jordin said. "I don't want to see either of you hurt."

Bree eyed her friend and wondered why Jordin seemed worried about her relationship with Austin. Especially since she initially seemed to be pushing her toward him. Bree had no doubt that Jordin's dinner party had been engineered to introduce them.

After Garland left, she stayed behind to talk to Jordin.

"Hey, something's bothering me," Bree said. "Do you think I'm making a mistake by spending time with your brother?"

"No, of course not. Why would you ask me that?"

Bree shrugged. "I don't know…it was something in your eyes, and then you suggested that we take things slow."

"I only meant that you've both gone through a lot. I *want* you two to be together, Bree. I think you're perfect for each other."

Bree picked up her purse. "I just wanted to be sure because I really like him." Breaking into a smile, she added, "The truth is that I'm crazy about Austin."

The weekend had come and gone. She'd gone to the movies Saturday night with Austin and they'd had a great time together. She really enjoyed his company.

Bree had ended her call with a colleague and was about to head to the kitchen to make blackened salmon for dinner when her cell phone rang again. Her heartbeat quickened when she saw it was Austin.

What was that shivering about? she wondered. Why was she reacting this way to his phone call?

She clicked on her phone. "Hello?"

"Hey, how was your day?"

Bree wished that he didn't sound as good as he looked. Or that when he had arrived to pick her up for dinner last night, he'd not been dressed as though he'd jumped off the page of a men's fashion magazine. Austin always showed impeccable manners by escorting her to his car and opening the door for her. However, it wasn't his manners she appreciated the most.

It was those sexy eyes and handsome face that had

taken her breath away. Bree sighed softly now as the memory rushed through her mind. Only then did she recall the question he had just asked her. "It was fine." Bree nibbled on her bottom lip. "How was yours?"

"My day was good," he responded. "I'm glad it's over, though. Right now, I just want to relax."

"You sound tired. We can cancel tonight if you want."

"No, I want to see you," Austin said. "But if you don't mind, I'd like to just stay in. You can come over here or I'll come to your place—it's up to you. It won't be a late night."

"Just come over here," she responded. "Emery is with Miss Sara. Would you like me to cook something?"

"No, I'll pick up dinner for us."

"Great… I guess I'll see you later, then."

Two hours later Bree opened the door to let Austin inside.

They stood staring at one another with longing. There was no denying that they shared an intense physical awareness of each other.

Without warning, he swung her into the circle of his arms, holding her snugly. He kissed her, sending her stomach into a wild swirl.

Austin's kiss was surprisingly gentle, yet it sent a brief shiver rippling through Bree. She buried her face against the corded muscles of his chest. She had no desire to back out of his embrace.

"I'm so glad you're here."

He gazed down at her with tenderness. "I will be here for as long as you need me."

Parting her lips, Bree raised herself on tiptoe, touching her lips to his.

His lips pressed against hers, then gently covered her

mouth. The kiss sent the pit of Bree's stomach into a wild swirl.

Austin showered her with kisses around her lips and along her jaw. As he roused her passion, his own grew stronger.

This time it was Bree who slowly pulled away. She took him by the hand and led him over to the sofa. She settled back, enjoying the feel of his arms around her.

They sat like this for a while before Bree rose to her feet, saying, "We'd better eat before the food gets cold."

Austin stood up and followed her to the dining room table.

She pulled the containers out of a plastic bag.

They made small talk while they ate.

"Watching Jordin get married—it reminded me of how much I miss being a wife."

Austin wiped at a fleck of food on her cheek. "Do you ever think about getting married again?"

"You want the truth?" she asked.

Austin nodded.

"I definitely want to get married again. To be honest… since I met you, I've been thinking about how long it's been since I've been this close to a man. How long it's been since I've kissed a man or made love." She raised her eyes to meet his. "It's been a while."

"Same here," Austin murmured.

"Just so you know… I'm not trying to seduce you," Bree interjected quickly. "I'm just being honest."

"I appreciate that."

She chuckled. "You look a little disappointed." Deep down, Bree had to fight her own overwhelming need to be close to him.

"Just a little," Austin murmured.

They found a movie on television to distract them from what they were feeling.

Bree made popcorn during a commercial break.

She didn't miss the way his gaze was riveted on her face, then moved over her body slowly. It was a definite turn-on.

Bree handed him the bowl, then reclaimed her seat beside him.

His arms encircled her, one hand in the small of her back. She relaxed, sinking into his cushioning embrace.

When the movie ended, Austin checked his watch and rose to his feet. "I'd better get going. It's getting late. I want you to know that I heard what you said and I respect that."

He brushed a gentle kiss across her forehead. "Good night, sweetheart."

She felt a certain sadness that their day was ending.

When he left, Bree jumped into the shower, hoping the stream of water would cool down the desire she felt deep within.

It was to no avail.

The fire Austin ignited in her refused to be extinguished.

Chapter 6

"I'm taking Emery to see the Fourth of July fireworks tonight," Bree announced over the phone. "I would invite you to join us, but…"

"I understand, sweetheart," Austin said. Deep down he felt a wave of disappointment. This was going to be his son's first time seeing the fireworks display and Austin wouldn't be there to share it with him.

"So, what are you doing today?"

"Uncle Jacques is hosting a cookout. I'm going to go there for a bit."

"I'm going to miss seeing you."

"Same here," he responded. "But we're still on for Saturday, right?"

"Actually, I promised Emery that we'd have pizza and go see a movie. I'm sorry."

"You have nothing to apologize for," Austin said. "A friend of mine is getting married at the end of the month. I'd like for you to be my plus one. The wedding's in Phoenix, Arizona, though. I know you have Emery… Are you able to get away?"

The thought of going away with him was tantalizing, the anticipation almost unbearable. "I'd love to go."

"Great. I'll book a two-bedroom suite for us."

"I'd appreciate that." Bree tried to ignore the smoldering flame burning through her. Austin was a temptation that she found hard to resist, but she wasn't about to turn down a chance to spend the weekend with him.

The following week, Austin worked until late in the evening, preparing for a case. He missed spending time with Bree, but spoke with her almost daily.

Her schedule was also hectic, but he loved that she made sure to leave her office early enough to have dinner with her son most nights. He knew she had an evening group therapy session once a week.

Austin stared at the stack of documents on his desk and sighed. He was in for another late night at the office.

"Knock knock…"

He glanced up at the entrance and smiled. "What are you doing here?"

"I thought I'd bring you something to eat," Bree responded.

He rose to his feet and crossed the floor in quick strides. Austin kissed her. "Thank you."

"I also wanted to see you, if only for a few minutes. I need to get home to Emery."

Austin smiled. "I'm glad you came by."

"I wish I could stay longer, but I really have to go."

He nodded in understanding, while hiding his disappointment.

Bree planted a kiss on his cheek. "Call me later."

"I won't be leaving here until after eleven or so. I'll call you tomorrow."

She glanced over at his desk. "Have fun."

"Yeah," Austin muttered.

Austin and Bree checked into the Alexander-DePaul Hotel in Phoenix. He was relieved when the plane finally landed in Arizona.

Austin sat down in one of the overstuffed chairs. "This is a nice suite."

Staring out a window, Bree agreed. "I just saw the shower in my bathroom and it can fit at least three people in it."

"What are you suggesting, sweetheart?" Austin asked. His gaze was riveted on her face, then moved over her body slowly.

"*Mr. DuGrandpre*, get your mind out of the gutter." Bree found herself extremely conscious of his virile appeal.

Rising to his feet, Austin chuckled. "You were the one who painted this picture in my head." Joining her at the window, he swung her into the circle of his arms. "Not to mention, I'm in this luxury suite with a very beautiful and sexy woman."

He kissed Bree, sending the pit of her stomach into a wild swirl. His lips seared a path down her neck, her shoulders, with tantalizing persuasion.

There was a knock on the door.

She glanced over at him. "Are you expecting someone?"

Nodding, Austin got up and crossed the room in quick strides. "I ordered some lunch for us."

He opened the door to allow the waiter to enter, pushing a cart.

She rose to her feet, moving to stand beside him.

Bree smiled. "Wow. You are full of surprises."

"I heard your stomach growling when we got off the plane," Austin teased.

She elbowed him in the arm as they silently observed the waiter as he placed their dinner on the table.

"So, what are we having?" Bree whispered.

"For starters, we're having seared scallops with bacon, Mediterranean salad and garlic brick chicken."

She rubbed her hands together. "Sounds delicious."

He loved that she was so easy to please.

Austin signed the check and gave the waiter a twenty-dollar tip.

They sat down at the dining table to eat.

He quickly blessed the food before they dived in.

Bree could feel him watching her. "Shouldn't you be concentrating on your food?" she asked.

"I can't believe we're here like this," he confessed. Austin's eyes traveled over her face and then slid downward. "I'm glad we are, though."

"I'm glad, too." Bree wiped her mouth with the edge of her napkin. "It's nice to get away every now and then. I had a crazy week, so this is perfect timing for me."

He stuck a forkful of food into his mouth and chewed slowly. Austin swallowed, then said, "I agree. I enjoy mini vacations."

She took a sip of her ice water. "Another thing we have in common."

"I guess there's nothing left for us to do except get married."

Bree laughed. "Definitely."

The air around them suddenly seemed electrified.

After they finished eating, she pushed away from the table and stood up. "Lunch was amazing," she murmured. "Now I'm going to have to spend the rest of the afternoon in the gym."

"Why don't you get a massage instead?" Austin suggested. "I've scheduled one for you later this afternoon."

"You're too good to me," she murmured.

"This view is incredible," Bree told Austin as they sat out on the balcony, watching the moon and stars. "I could sit here for hours just looking at the stars in the sky and at the city below."

He took a sip of his hot tea. "I could sit here all night watching you."

She stretched and yawned.

"Uh-huh…"

She glanced over at Austin. "Uh-huh *what*?"

"It's past midnight," he announced. "We should probably go to bed." Although he wasn't ready for the evening to end, Austin could tell that Bree was tired.

"But we're having such a good time together." She yawned a second time.

"And you can barely keep your eyes open. Let me walk you to your room." A shiver of wanting ran down Austin's spine. He moved toward her, impelled involuntarily by his own passion.

Bree shook her head. "I can make it across the hall by myself," she told him. "If you walk me over there—I know that I won't be strong enough to let you come back to your own room. I'll see you in the morning."

When she left, Austin headed to the bathroom. He was in desperate need of a cold shower.

Bree took an instant dislike to everything she had packed for the trip and now wished that she had gone shopping earlier.

After her shower, Bree changed into an emerald-green Tadashi dress.

"This is so not me," she mumbled as she stared at her reflection in the floor-length mirror.

Next, she slipped on another dress that she'd snagged on sale at a boutique the day before they left Charleston.

"Not bad," she whispered.

Bree changed again, this time into a Vera Wang silk halter dress in a vivid purple color. She slipped on a pair of silver-and-amethyst jeweled sandals with straps that wrapped around her ankles. Bree added an amethyst ring, white gold and amethyst bangles with matching earrings to complete her look.

She placed makeup on her face with a light touch.

Bree smiled as she looked at herself in the mirror, satisfied with what she saw.

She glanced at her watch.

She had twenty minutes, and the last thing she had to do was her hair. She undid her twists and fingered through her hair, combing through the waves.

Bree could hear Austin moving about in the living room and wondered how he would respond when she stepped outside the bedroom.

His gaze gave her body a timeless sweep and she felt her heartbeat quicken.

"You look stunning," he said.

"Thanks. You look nice yourself."

They were soon on their way to the wedding location.

He backed out of the driveway. "I have to warn you that Will and Jade are a unique couple."

"I don't think I'm going to be too surprised. In my line of work, I've come to meet some *different* people," she said, noticing the smooth sound of the SUV's engine as he drove down the street.

Austin brought the car to a stop at a traffic light.

"How long have you known Will?" Bree questioned.

"Since high school. I've known Jade since law school. I introduced them when he came for my graduation."

They pulled up for valet parking.

Bree noted the immaculate building with a backdrop of mountains that housed the hotel. The architecture probably dated back to the eighteen hundreds, she decided. "Nice."

"It's an old hotel. The owners renovated it a few years ago—Will was one of the interior designers."

Austin offered her his arm, which she took. He had brought her here with him tonight and she intended to enjoy herself.

Austin escorted Bree into the hotel. As they neared the ballroom, she slowed her steps, surveying poster-size drawings of the bride and groom.

"Will drew them," he said.

"He did a great job."

Two tall statues of women stood on either side of the door.

"Oh, my goodness," she whispered. "Austin, they're real people. She blinked."

At the sound of a harpist playing, he said, "We'd better take our seats."

They were seated three rows from the front.

Bree glanced down at the wedding program and chuckled. The front read: *So, You're Going to Sit Through a Wedding: A Practical Guide to Not Falling Asleep.*

"I have to warn you that Will and Jade are very unconventional," Austin whispered. "So, expect just about anything with this wedding."

"Okay," she said.

Bree glanced around, noting that several people seated on the end of the row had flowers in hand. It was not something she was used to seeing at weddings. *This is going to be interesting.*

The bridesmaids, dressed in a vivid rainbow of colors, made their entrance.

Jade made her grand entrance on the arm of her father. She stopped to collect the flowers, building her bouquet along the way to the altar.

When it was time for the bride and groom to say their vows, they played rock, paper and scissors to determine who would go first in saying their vows.

Bree chuckled.

"I told you," Austin whispered. "You never know what to expect with these two."

Jade won and spoke first. "Long ago you were just a dream for me. Thank you for being what you are to me. I love, honor and protect you. Will, I give you my heart for eternity, my friend and my love."

Bree's eyes grew wet. She blinked rapidly to keep her tears from falling.

It was Will's turn to speak. "Jade, I love you, baby. Through all the uncertainties and trials of the present and future, I promise to be faithful to you and love you as long as we both shall live."

Austin reached over and took her hand in his.

The bride and groom exchanged rings and before the pastor could get the words out of his mouth, Will captured Jade's lips with his own.

Laughter and applause erupted around the room.

"I present to you all, Mr. and Mrs. William Manning."

More applause followed.

Wedding guests were led to another room across the hall for the reception. The soft glow of the candles high-lighted the hues of purple, teal, orange and traces of gold in the tablecloths. Each table featured edible centerpieces on marble slabs of cascading cheese, cracker and fruit. Marinated olives were placed in stoneware on each table for guests to savor.

"The ceremony was unique but beautiful," Bree said.

Austin wrapped an arm around her. "I like the idea of the human statues."

She flashed him a grin. "It was definitely a nice touch. People can't stop talking about them."

He pulled a chair out for her at their designated table.

Bree sat down.

Austin sat down next to her. "Thanks for coming with me."

"It's been a nice little getaway." She ran her fingers through her hair. "I needed a break."

"I know you miss Emery."

She nodded. "I do. I called to check on him earlier and he hurt my feelings a little. He was watching *The LEGO Movie* and didn't have time to talk to me."

"I'm sure when you call back, he will be more than ready to have a conversation with you."

Bree placed her hand in his. "Thank you for saying that."

"Would you like to dance?" Austin asked her.

"I love dancing. I just haven't done it in a long time," she said, taking him by the hand.

Bree walked slowly, her body swaying to the music. "I *love* this song."

Austin escorted her to the middle of the dance floor and began dancing to the music.

One song ended and another began while they were still on the dance floor.

They left the reception right after the bride and groom departed.

Back at the hotel, Bree made a cup of green tea with co-

conut and enjoyed the beautiful view of downtown Phoenix out the hotel window. She took a deep breath, then sipped her tea, hoping it would stop her heart from hammering.

The erratic pounding in her chest had started when Austin had removed his shirt as he strolled across the carpet to the other bedroom. It was as if knowing they were under the same roof and breathing the same air was getting to her.

Separating the two bedrooms was a spacious living room, workspace and dining area, but being in the same suite with such a handsome man... Bree took another deep breath and exhaled slowly.

Trying to put thoughts of Austin out of her mind, she turned back to the view.

There's a full moon tonight. It's so beautiful... I could stand here all night looking at it.

The hotel was in the thick of downtown and the surrounding buildings were massive and numerous, but she still had a beautiful view of the mountains.

"Bree?"

She gasped at the sound of her name and turned from the window.

Austin stood naked except for his pajama pants, which rode low on his hips, looking sexier than he had earlier that night.

"Yes?"

"Why aren't you in bed?"

His masculine scent reached out to Bree, sending her entire body into a heated tailspin.

"I thought you were sleeping," she said, trying to stay in control.

A slow smile touched his lips and her body tingled in response.

The erratic pounding in her chest returned.

Had it truly ever left?

"I couldn't sleep." He rubbed a hand over his face. "You should probably try to get some rest. We have an early flight in the morning."

Bree glanced down at her empty cup and came up with the perfect excuse to leave the living room. "I've finished my tea. Maybe sleep will come now."

When she walked past him, Austin reached out, taking the cup from her hand and placing it on the end table before wrapping a strong arm around her waist and pulling her to him.

His head lowered to hers.

Soon she was kissing him as hungrily as he was kissing her. Bree molded her body to his as if it was the most natural thing, and instinctively wrapped her arms around his neck. Desire felt like talons sinking into her skin, spreading through her body in a heated rush, making her moan deep in her throat.

Bree reluctantly broke off the kiss and unwrapped her arms from his neck before taking in a deep breath. "Self-control, girl," she whispered.

"What did you say, sweetheart?" he asked, dipping his head low to hers.

She stared up into his penetrating, chestnut-brown eyes and wondered if Austin had any idea that they were an aphrodisiac. Just staring into their depths caused crazy things to happen to her.

"Bree?" he prompted.

She recalled he had asked her a question and decided to be honest. "I'm trying to talk myself out of taking something that I want."

He lifted a brow. "Really?"

"Yes."

He placed his hand on her shoulder. "Keep talking. Maybe you can convince us both."

Bree kissed him on the cheek. "Good night, Austin."

His lips curved into a smile. "I'll see you in the morning, sweetheart."

Chapter 7

The August weather was nice and warm, perfect for a day on the golf course. Austin spent the morning with his father at the country club in Charleston trying to learn the game.

He was a novice and found the game was not as easy as he first imagined. "I hope I'm not embarrassing you too much," he said.

Etienne laughed. "You need to learn how to hold the golf club the proper way. That's part of the problem. Keep your grip light."

Austin did as his father instructed, but his heart wasn't in it. He wanted to shout for joy when the lesson came to an end.

On the way to the car, Etienne said, "I want you to know that I'm very proud of the man you've become, Austin."

"You're not just saying that because I became a lawyer, are you?"

He chuckled. "You've heard the whole DuGrandpre legacy story."

Austin nodded. "From Grandfather when he came to visit. He sent me brochures from the top law schools."

"My father had a grand vision of building a family of lawyers. He never seemed to understand that not everyone in the family shared that vision."

"Was there something else you wanted to do?"

"When I was younger, I wanted to be in law enforcement. I pictured myself an FBI man, but my father—he was against the very idea. I didn't want to disappoint him, so I studied law. It wasn't until I started law school that I developed a passion for it. I think my father knew all along that this is where I belonged."

Etienne looked at Austin. "How about you?"

"I wanted to be a forensic psychologist or a profiler." He chuckled. "I guess I thought of myself as an FBI man, as well."

"Like father like son…"

Austin nodded. "I guess so."

"How's your love life?"

"It's funny you bring this up," Austin responded. "I've met someone I really like."

"Good. When do we get to meet her?"

"You already have, Dad. It's Jordin's friend Bree."

"Ah…the beautiful Dr. Collins. She has a little boy, you know? You have to want the whole package if you expect to have a relationship with her."

Austin nodded. "I'm looking forward to meeting her son."

"How long have you two been dating?"

"A couple of months now, which is why I haven't met Emery, but I really like her."

"Are you ready to settle down?"

"I am," Austin responded. "If I wait too much longer, I'll be too old to teach my children how to play anything other than golf."

Etienne laughed. "I guess that'll fall on me."

"Dad, I hate this game."

"Tell me this. How do you feel about bowling?"

"Now you're speaking my language," Austin said. "I know how to bowl and I'm pretty good at it."

"Let's get out of here," Etienne suggested. "They have a fantastic buffet at the country club."

Minutes later they were seated at a table dining on garlic lime chicken, grilled asparagus with lime dressing, four-cheese mashed potatoes with wild mushrooms and onion bread.

"The chef outdid herself," Etienne whispered to him.

Austin agreed. He sliced off a piece of the tender chicken and stuck it into his mouth, savoring the flavor. "Everything is delicious."

After lunch, he drove home to shower and change. He was meeting up with Bree in a couple of hours. Although he was trying to be patient, Austin wanted to meet Emery. He appreciated the information from Jordin and the tidbits shared by Bree, but he desired to meet the little boy.

Austin hummed softly as he pulled into the parking garage connected to the building where he lived.

Inside the condo, Austin walked straight to the bathroom. He showered, slipped into a robe and settled down in the sitting room to watch television. He had enough time to relax before his date.

He lay back with his eyes closed, dreaming of the day when he and Emery could hang out as father and son.

Bree spent the day with Emery, painting in the park.

"Lookit, Mommy. Look at my picture."

"Honey, it's beautiful. Is that the house over there?"

He nodded. "I made it for you."

Her cell phone rang.

"Hey, girl," Jordin greeted. "Emery's still staying with us tonight, right?"

"Yes. Thanks for this. I'm not ready for him to meet Austin yet. I need to see where this relationship is going."

There was a slight pause, then Jordin responded, "Not a problem. Ethan and I love having him with us. We're practicing for our own child."

"Really? You guys are trying to get pregnant?"

"Yeah. I'm looking forward to starting a family."

"I think it's wonderful, Jordin."

"You're cooking a romantic dinner tonight at your house…hmmm… Are you planning for this to turn into a sleepover?"

Bree chuckled. "It's just dinner. We're not at the point for sleepovers."

They talked a few minutes more before ending the call.

She and Emery stayed another half hour at the park.

"We need to pack your bag," Bree said when they arrived home. "Auntie Jordin is coming to pick you up soon."

"Yeah…"

"Which pajamas do you want to sleep in? Batman or Spider-Man?"

"Ninja Tuttles," he uttered.

Emery put his hands to his face and cracked up with laughter.

"You're so silly." Her heart was so full of love for the little boy crawling around on the floor. "My silly little man."

"Mommy, I love you."

"I love you more, baby."

Once his bag was packed, Bree gave him a bath.

He was dressed and impatient by the time Jordin arrived.

"Girl, he thought you weren't coming," Bree said. "He

asked me at least twenty times when you were going to get here."

"Oh, honey, Auntie's sorry for running late. My dad came over and we were talking. I'm sorry."

"I okay now." Emery reached for her hand. "Can we go?"

"You're ready to leave Mommy?"

He nodded. "I be back."

Bree kissed him. "Have fun with Auntie Jordin and Uncle Ethan."

Jordin glanced over at her. "*You* have fun tonight."

Austin knocked on Bree's front door shortly after eight. He had stopped to pick up Thai food for them.

"You look beautiful," he whispered, making Bree's heart swell.

"How did your golf lesson go?" She walked into the kitchen and took a couple of plates from the cabinet.

"We're going to go bowling next time. I had to break down and tell my dad that I have no interest whatsoever in golf. It's just not for me."

"How did he take it?"

"Very well," Austin stated. "I got the impression that he isn't that crazy about the sport, either."

They dined on a spicy shrimp soup, red chicken curry and fried rice.

"You look beautiful," Austin murmured in her ear. "In case I haven't told you already."

"You mentioned it."

Their feet moved to the slow rhythm of "If I Was Your Man," while Austin pulled her firmly against him. The heat of his skin radiated through his white shirt, warming her in the evening cool. Her eyes closed as his fingers tightened around hers, and Bree rested her head against his shoulder.

The song ended and they pulled apart.

As if going with instinct, Austin refused to relinquish her hand as she started to step away. Instead he gave it a gentle tug, pulling her back into his arms. He smiled, his teeth flashing in the candlelight.

He kissed her.

They smiled at each other a long time, until Austin quietly commented, "This feels nice...being here with you like this."

"I agree," she murmured.

"I want more nights like this."

Bree's eyes widened in surprise. "I'm not quite sure what you mean by that."

"I'm not one for partying and hanging at the club. I like what we did tonight—a quiet dinner and dancing." Austin looked at her. "I hope it didn't just get weird between us."

"It didn't." She picked another chocolate-covered strawberry off the platter. "I asked because I don't like to assume."

Austin poured white wine into the glasses, then handed one to her.

"Thank you." Bree took a sip. "I was never much into clubbing. I know it sounds strange since Caleb was a musician. The only time I ever went to a club was when he performed."

He was staring at one of the photos of Emery, prompting a smile on her lips. "I would introduce you, but I don't want to rush it. I hope you understand. Maybe I'm overprotective, but I want his life to have the consistency that mine didn't. Having him get attached to someone and then lose him..."

"You're doing the right thing. He doesn't need to meet every man you date."

"I'm glad we're on the same page, Austin."

"I will meet him one day," he responded. "I don't plan on going anywhere."

"I must admit that I like the sound of that, because I'm not looking for a casual relationship. I'm more of the marrying type."

"Once again, we're on the same page."

Instead of going home, Austin drove to the neighborhood where Jordin and Ethan lived.

He wanted a glimpse of his son.

"Austin, is something wrong?"

"I'm sorry for coming by so late, but I wanted to see Emery. I know he's sleeping and I promise I won't wake him. I just need to see him for myself."

He followed her upstairs to the room where Emery lay sleeping.

His heart filled and overflowed with love as his gaze soaked up the sight of his son for the first time. Austin wanted a closer look, but dared not take the chance of disturbing him. He remained in the doorway for a few minutes before returning downstairs.

He found Jordin in the kitchen, making a cup of tea.

"It's hard to believe that my little boy is in there sleeping. I still can't tell who he resembles most."

"He's a cutie." Jordin gestured toward the Keurig. "Would you like some tea or coffee?"

"I'm fine."

They heard the garage door going up.

"Ethan's home," Jordan announced. "I know you don't want too many people knowing, but I think it's time we told him about Emery. I don't like keeping secrets from him. You don't have to worry. He's very discreet."

"That's fine."

Ethan entered the house through the garage. "Hey…

Austin, I didn't know you were here. I thought you were seeing Bree tonight."

Jordin planted a quick kiss on Ethan's lips. "We need to tell you something, honey."

He looked from his wife to Austin. "What's going on?"

"Emery's my biological son."

"Excuse me?"

"My ex-girlfriend never told me about the baby. She left town when we broke up, then had the baby and gave him up for adoption. After a long search, I've learned that Bree was the adopter."

Ethan's shock was written all over his face. "Does Bree know?"

"Not yet." Austin glanced over at his sister, then said, "I plan to tell her."

"You should've told her before you two got involved."

"I told him to wait," Jordin confessed. "I know Bree and this is not something she's going to handle well. It's better that she gets to know Austin first."

"Okay, I get that," Ethan said, "but your brother's dating her. If you prolong this, I don't think it's going to end well."

"I intend to tell Bree when the time is right."

"Honey, no one else knows about this," Jordin interjected. "Just the three of us."

"I won't say a word, but I think you both need to talk to Bree before she finds out another way."

When Ethan went upstairs, Austin glanced at his sister. "Your husband's not happy about this."

"He doesn't like secrets," Jordin stated.

"I don't, either. I hate keeping Bree in the dark like this, but I need to gain her trust. I need her as an advocate and not an enemy when I go back to court. Although Emery is my son, the courts can decide not to reverse the adoption."

"Would that be so bad?"

"Jordin, if that happens, I won't have any say in my son's life. If things with Bree go sour—I could lose him and I'm not going to let that happen. I intend to make sure no one will be able to just take Emery from me again."

"I understand what you're saying, Austin." Jordin paused a moment before asking, "I need to know something. Do you really care for Bree?"

"Of course I do."

"She doesn't deserve to be played."

"My feelings for her are genuine, Jordin. You don't have anything to worry about, sis." Austin rose to his feet. "Thanks for the coffee and for letting me see Emery. I'm going to leave so you and your hubby can talk."

"You and Bree are good for each other. I want this to work out for all of you."

"So do I," he muttered.

Jordin walked him to the door. "I'll see you tomorrow."

Back at his condo, Austin paced the living room floor. He wasn't so sure that he'd handled this situation with Bree the right way. Maybe it was better to put some distance between them.

He put his hands to his face. *Did I handle this all wrong?*

Maybe it would be better to end things with her now, Austin thought sadly. He had fallen in love with her and the idea of walking away pained him.

Chapter 8

He'd made his decision.

Austin was on his way to see Bree. He was going to tell her everything before they went to dinner. He didn't think it wise to discuss such a sensitive topic in a public place.

She was at her office and requested that he pick her up from there. Her neighbor's car was disabled, so she'd let Sara use her vehicle.

"Sweetheart, can we talk?" Austin asked when he arrived. Her staff had already left for the day, so they were alone in the office.

"Sure," she responded while peering into her computer. "There's something I need to discuss with you. I just need to make a quick note in this file and then I'm done."

Moments later she turned off her computer screen and joined him on the sofa.

Austin reached over and took her hand in his. "Bree, we've been together for a few months now, but I feel like I've known you forever."

She smiled. "I feel the same way about you. That's why I wanted to talk to you. You've become very important to me, Austin. Because of that, I think it's time you met my son."

He was surprised by her words. "Are you sure?"

Bree gave a slight nod. "I'm positive. Instead of going out, why don't we eat in...the three of us. Emery doesn't have a father figure in his life. As much as I love him, I can't teach Emery how to be a man. He needs a positive role model. It should be you, Austin."

He kissed her.

"I promise I will be here for you and Emery. Nothing will ever change that. I can't put into words how much I care about you." Austin held her close. He was finally going to meet his son. To tell her now would likely change that—it wasn't a risk he was willing to take.

"Thanks for watching Emery, Miss Sara."

"It's my pleasure. You know how much I love that li'l boy. He's just so precious." Her gaze traveled to Austin. "Now, who is this handsome man?"

"This is Austin DuGrandpre."

"Whose son are you?"

"Etienne," he responded.

She seemed pleased with his response. "He represented my father several years ago. Your daddy is a good man."

The moment had finally arrived for father to finally come face-to-face with his son.

A little curly-haired boy burst into the room. "Mommy..." He peered at Austin and slowed his steps.

"Sweetie, I want you to meet someone," Bree said. "This is Austin. He's your aunt Jordin's brother and he's having dinner with us tonight. Can you say hello?"

"Hel-lo..." He clung to her like a lifeline.

Austin felt an instant's squeezing hurt. He reminded himself that this was their first meeting. Bree had mentioned in conversation that Emery was shy when it came to meeting new people.

He kneeled so that he was eye level with his son. "I hear that you like Batman. Superman, the Hulk and Ninja Turtles."

Emery smiled. "Spider-Man."

"I like him, too."

The little boy looked up at Bree in expectation.

"Austin," she said.

"Au'tin."

He blinked rapidly to keep his tears from falling. Austin spied a Spider-Man toy on the floor in the family room. "Hey, why don't you show me your superheroes?"

"'Kay..." Smiling, Emery went off to his room.

"You know he's going to bring out every toy he has," Bree said with a soft chuckle.

"I'll help clean up."

She seemed surprised by his words.

"I'm serious," Austin stated. "I love playing superheroes. When I was a little boy, I wanted to be Superman."

"C'mon Au'tin."

"I'm coming, buddy." He winked at Bree before walking briskly to join Emery in his bedroom. This was the moment Austin had been dreaming of since he first found out about the little boy.

Joy, like a sunburst, went off inside Bree as she watched the man who had come to mean so much to her spending time with her son.

She could hear them laughing and talking while she prepared dinner. Bree counted herself fortunate to have Austin in her life. Her feelings for him grew stronger each day. There was a time when she refused to even consider the idea of marrying again, but now, she found herself looking forward to the future—hopefully one that included Austin.

The trio enjoyed dinner together. Afterward, Austin and Emery settled into the family room while Bree cleaned the kitchen.

Fifteen minutes later, Bree entered the room, pausing to watch Emery pushing a car toward Austin. She was amazed at how good he was with children. She felt a moment's sadness that she couldn't have a child with him. He would be a great father.

Slow down, girl.

Austin looked up at her and smiled.

She returned it with one of her own. "Looks like you two really hit it off. Whatever you were doing really cracked Emery up."

"He was Thor and I was the Hulk. I'm afraid he knocked me out with his hammer. More than once."

Emery played with Austin for another hour before Bree put him to bed.

Austin watched them from the doorway. It was obvious how much she loved Emery.

They returned to the kitchen for dessert.

Seated at the table with Austin, Bree pushed her plate away and asked, "So, what do you think of my little boy?"

"I'm in love." The words were out of his mouth before Austin realized that he'd said them. "He's such a good kid. I love his personality."

She wiped her mouth on the edge of her napkin before saying, "I noticed that it was like you couldn't take your eyes off him. I've seen you with Ryker's children, but the way you look at Emery...it's just different."

"Maybe it's because I'm crazy about his mother." His gaze was riveted on her face. "I love you, Bree."

She opened her mouth to speak, but no words came out.

Did he just say the L word?

"Please tell me that I didn't hear you wrong. Can you say it again please?"

Austin smiled. "I love you."

Impelled by her own emotions, Bree got up and walked around the table to where he was sitting.

He pushed his chair away from the table.

She sat down on his lap.

Gathering her into his arms, Austin held her snugly. "This feels so right to me," he whispered.

"I love you, too."

After putting the dishes in the dishwasher, they left the kitchen and settled down in her family room.

Austin kissed her, his tongue sending shivers of desire racing through her.

Bree matched him kiss for kiss.

He slowly pulled away, saying, "It's getting late and I have to be in court first thing in the morning."

She groaned in protest.

"I'll see you tomorrow," he whispered in her ear.

Bree wrapped her arms around him. "I don't want you to leave."

"I don't want to leave," Austin responded honestly. "But it's best that I do. I don't think you're ready to take our relationship to the next level."

"I haven't been with anyone since Caleb. My body tells me to keep you here by any means necessary, but I appreciate you for not pressing the matter."

He tightened his embrace, drawing her as close.

"When we make love, I want you to have no shadows across your heart." Austin lowered his lips to hers and kissed her. "Until you're ready... I'll wait."

"You're too good to be true, Austin DuGrandpre."

* * *

The world was suddenly a much brighter place as far as Austin was concerned. He was in love with a wonderful woman and getting to know his son was an amazing experience.

Briefcase in hand, he made his way toward the elevators.

He was soon joined by a colleague. "Graham, I heard you and Judge Walsh had words yesterday."

Patting his blazer pocket, he said, "My checkbook's a little lighter as a result. It's gonna probably cost me money every time I walk into that man's courtroom."

"You might want to set aside some cash, then," Austin responded with a grin. "I hear that he's not the one to mess with."

Graham shrugged. "Walsh needs to retire. He's been around since I was a little boy. And he was old then."

Laughing, the two men stepped off the elevator when the doors opened.

Austin waved at the receptionist as he walked passed her desk. He continued through the doors, which led to the office area.

Rochelle DuGrandpre walked out of her office, heading straight for him. He groaned inwardly.

"Good morning, Aunt Rochelle."

"You know, I didn't think you'd still be here, Austin, but I was wrong."

"Why did you think that?"

"I figured your mama would've convinced you to go back to Dallas. Irene never liked you spending too much time with us."

Austin kept his temper in check. "I'm a grown man capable of making my own decisions."

She smiled. "You sound just like Ryker. I hope you

boys understand that mothers do whatever we have to do
to protect our children."

"It doesn't go unnoticed, Aunt Rochelle."

She leaned and whispered, "You have no idea how
much it pleases your father to have you here in this firm.
It is a dream come true for him."

"It means a lot to me, as well."

Rochelle nodded in approval. "You have a nice day,
Austin."

"You, too."

He poked his head into Jadin's office. "Good morning…"

"Morning," she responded, her eyes glued to the computer monitor, engrossed in her work.

The next office was his.

Austin sat at his desk and opened his calendar, reviewing his appointments for the day.

His eyes traveled the room, imagining photographs of
Emery scattered around. His first-grade picture…first
football team photo and a host of others. They would share
many firsts together—something he never had with his
father.

The way he and Bree connected brought everything together perfectly. Austin knew she was a devoted mom—
he wanted her to see him as the perfect father for Emery.
This way, when everything came out, she would not feel
threatened.

Austin entered Bree's house, grinning from ear to ear.

"You're up to something. What is it?"

He held up three tickets.

"What are those?" Bree inquired.

"Tickets to the Children's Museum of the Low Country on Saturday. Have you been there?"

"No, we haven't. I'd planned to take Emery before the summer ended, so this is perfect."

She was beyond touched by his gesture.

"Make yourself comfortable," Bree told him. "I need to wake up Emery from his nap."

Austin ventured into the kitchen.

The radio was playing softly and the table was set for three. On the counter was a slow cooker. He lifted the lid and the appetizing smell of chili wafted out.

His stomach rumbled in appreciation.

"What are you doing?"

Turning around to face her, Austin responded, "I was drawn here by a tantalizing aroma. I wanted to see what it was."

"Or you're just hungry."

He laughed. "That, too."

Emery ran into the kitchen.

"Hey, buddy," Austin greeted. "What are you up to?"

"I was sleepin'."

"Little boys need a lot of rest."

"So I can be strong?"

He nodded.

"Au'tin, I happy at you here."

Bree felt a catch beneath her ribs at the pleasure Austin and Emery found in one another. Tears pricked at her eyelids. A deep, tearing need took her breath, and she turned back toward the slow cooker.

Austin was almost too good to be true. She could not imagine anything more perfect than the way things were going with him. This was the first time there were no warning bells going off in her head.

Emery picked up the television remote in the family room. She soon heard the familiar Spider-Man movie. Her son watched it almost daily.

She heard footsteps in the kitchen, but didn't turn around.

Bree felt his arms around her and leaned into him. Austin's nearness had an arousing effect on her. "Dinner's ready," she murmured, struggling to keep her focus on what she was doing.

Chapter 9

Austin invited Bree to join him for a charity event chaired by Eleanor DuGrandpre. When they entered the ballroom, the crowd seemed to part for her as if in a series of orchestrated moves. He had to admit that she was electrifying. Her hair, her eyes and the way her hips swayed when she walked. The hard tap of her heels against the marble floor sounded like tiny gunshots, even over the noise of the surrounding crush of people.

They found their table and sat down.

Eleanor walked over, plastering her best professional smile on her face. "I'm glad you two could make it. Have some champagne, look around at what our artists have to offer and enjoy yourself."

Austin watched his stepmother navigate through the crowd, charming men and women alike. It was obvious she loved this kind of stuff.

"What are you doing next Saturday?" Bree inquired. "Emery's birthday is Thursday, but we're celebrating over the weekend. We'd love for you to join us for the party at my house."

"I'd love to come." He was aware of his son's birthday and had already purchased a gift for him.

They moved about the room, eyeing the artwork.

"I love this one," Bree said. "It's perfect for my office."

"I notice you seem to love landscapes."

She nodded. "I do. I find that they promote calmness within my clients."

Austin pointed to a painting hanging nearby. "This one's nice."

"I like that one, too."

Jordin walked up to them. "Hey, you two. Found something you like?"

"I think I'm going to bid on this one," Bree stated. "It matches the other paintings in my office."

"Are you just getting here?" Austin asked his sister.

"Yeah. Ethan's flight was late."

"I'm having Emery's party on Saturday," Bree announced.

Jordin exchanged a quick look with her brother. "You know I'll be there for my sweetie."

"Can you believe he's already turning three? My baby is growing up so fast."

Austin embraced her. "He's still got a long way to go, babe. There may come a time when you can't wait for him to grow up."

Bree shook her head. "I don't think so. I dread the thought of him leaving me. I'm already praying he'll choose to stay close to home when it comes to college."

"She's serious," Jordin interjected. "Bree's been saying this since we were in school. She wants to keep her children close to her."

Austin took her hand. "It's a good thing for them to leave the nest, sweetheart."

"I know," she murmured. "I'm fine with them leaving—I just don't want my children spread out all over the country. I want to host family dinners like the ones your family has."

He understood why Bree felt this way. She didn't have family and while she didn't say much about it—he knew it bothered her.

She walked over to a painting a few feet away.

"I need to find my husband," Jordin said, looking around. "I see some pieces that would look great in our living room."

"Talk to you later, sis."

Austin joined Bree. "This is very nice."

"I love this one, too."

At the end of the evening, Austin handed his credit card to the cashier. "I'm paying for all three."

"You don't have to pay for mine," Bree said.

"I want to do this," he said. "I insist that you take the money and put it in Emery's education fund."

"Austin DuGrandpre, you never cease to amaze me."

"Au'tin, it my burtday."

"Happy birthday, buddy. Now, how old are you?"

"I tree."

"Three years old…wow. You are such a big boy."

"Hey, cousin," Ryker greeted. He gave Austin a knowing smile. "Looks like you and Bree are getting along well."

"We are."

"Emery obviously likes you."

"I like him, too."

Ryker asked in a low voice, "So, you thinking of settling down anytime soon?"

Austin simply smiled.

"Look at that…"

"What are you two up to?" Jordin inquired.

"We're not doing anything," Ryker answered, *"Little Miss Matchmaker."*

She broke into a grin. "Maybe I should open a dating service."

"Or you could come help your husband," Ethan suggested. He was standing in the doorway. "Kai and Amya just challenged us to a dance off."

Austin laughed. "You might as well give up now. Have you seen them dance lately?"

Ryker agreed. "Garland has them taking lessons and I have to admit—they're pretty good."

"Honey, c'mon. Let's go get our tails whipped. We're a team so we have to take this hit together."

Jordin chuckled. "I can't believe you're falling for this. I know I can dance. Let's go show these little girls how it's done."

Austin looked over at Bree. "I don't know about you, but I want to see this."

"Right behind you," she murmured. "I want to check on Emery first. They're a little too quiet in his room. Three boys…"

Bree walked in one direction and he in the other.

Austin watched in amusement as Ryker's daughters took to the floor, their moves flawless for a set of five-year-olds. He was loving this, being around family like this. He wanted Emery to experience this, as well—to be surrounded by love.

He leaned over and whispered, "Jordin, I think you and Ethan should give up now. These girls have a whole dance routine."

"I got this."

When Kai and Amya were done, Jordin looked at her husband and said, "You ready?"

"No, I think we should just declare them winners."

She broke into a grin. "I agree."

Austin heard Emery's laughter coming right at him. He pressed himself against the wall and waited until the sound was upon him. He reached out and grabbed the little boy. "You having a good time, buddy?"

"Yes. I have fun."

"Me, too, buddy. I'm having the time of my life."

The following weekend, Jordin had Emery spend Saturday night with her and Ethan because Austin had planned a special surprise for Bree.

"Where are we going?" she inquired.

"To the waterfront park."

She smiled. "For a moonlight walk?"

"That and more," he responded. "We're going to have a picnic near the Pineapple Fountain."

"How romantic."

The park faced the Charleston Harbor and Revenal Bridge and was one of their favorite places to visit.

Austin laid a blanket down on the grass for them to sit on.

They sat facing each other.

Bree accepted the plate from Austin. "This is a beautiful night."

He agreed.

"Did you make all this?" she asked.

Austin shook his head. "Aubrie actually put together the basket for me. I simply picked it up and put it in the car."

Bree laughed. "You're not even going to take credit... not even a little bit. I love your honesty."

Guilt filtered through him at her words. He still hadn't summoned up the courage to tell her the truth about Emery. Mostly because he feared losing Bree.

"What time should I be ready for the barbecue on Monday?" she asked.

"One o'clock."

"I missed the DuGrandpre Labor Day Barbecue last year," Bree stated. "Emery was sick, so we stayed home."

"I wasn't there, either. I went to Dallas to spend some time with my mom. This will be my first one."

"They do it up big, Austin."

"I'm looking forward to spending this one with you and Emery."

"This is nice," she said, her eyes traveling the park. "It's beautiful out here."

"I'm glad you like it," he responded. "I wasn't sure how this was going to turn out. They said it was going to rain."

"I'm glad it didn't," Bree stated. "I would've hated missing out on this. It's very romantic."

Austin wrapped an arm around her. "My life would be empty if it wasn't for you and Emery. I want you to know that."

"You don't ever have to worry about losing me. Whatever this is that's going on between us—I'm in a hundred percent."

Chapter 10

"Come in, Austin," Eleanor greeted warmly as she stepped aside to let him enter the house. "Everybody is outside on the patio."

"I can walk around to the back," he said.

"You'll do no such thing. Get on in here."

He embraced his stepmother. "You look beautiful as always."

"Boy, please... I haven't even combed my hair today."

Austin chuckled. "You can't tell."

After they settled at one of the picnic tables, Bree said, "I'll get your chicken off the grill. I know you're hungry."

"Thanks, babe."

She returned minutes later and placed the plate before him, heaped with mixed greens, chicken and macaroni salad.

"It was the last one ready. Ryker's putting more chicken on the grill, but since you talked about it on the way here, I figured I'd better grab a piece for you while some was still available."

Her cell phone rang.

"I need to take this call."

Bree returned, saying, "Honey, I have to go. One of my patients just tried to commit suicide and I need to see her."

"Do you want me to go with you?" Austin asked.

She shook her head. "No, you stay here with Emery. Fix me a plate, please."

He kissed her.

Austin walked her out to the car.

His father came from the back and said, "Take a walk with me, son."

"Sure."

"I'd like to talk to your mother," Etienne announced as they strolled toward the front of the house.

"Why?" Austin asked, stopping in his tracks. "The two of you haven't spoken in almost twenty-seven years."

"I wasn't a good husband, son. I'm sure she's told you this much."

He nodded. "I don't know the specifics and I don't need to know. It's not my business."

"I owe Irene an apology. As I'm getting on in years, I'm beginning to see things differently. I made some terrible choices in the past. One of those was hurting your mother."

"Dad, I don't think she's ready to have a conversation with you, but I'll pass on the message that you'd like to speak with her."

"Thank you, son. I'd really appreciate it."

"Did you ever love her?" Austin inquired. "Mom never believed you cared as much for her as she did for you."

"I loved your mother more than I can say, but we were young and we both let pride get in the way of trying to work things out. Then I met Eleanor."

"You don't owe me any explanations," Austin interjected. He didn't want to be in the middle of his parents' situation and he wasn't going to take sides again. He'd chosen his mother based on what she'd told him, then found out that it wasn't the complete truth.

Their conversation turned to sports.

"I'm looking forward to football season," said Etienne. "I think the Saints are going to have a good year."

Austin grinned. "I feel the same way about the Cowboys."

His father roared with laughter. "Son, you're dreaming. Besides, where is your loyalty? The DuGrandpres come from strong New Orleans roots."

"I like the Saints, but I grew up in Dallas. I love my Cowboys."

His stepmother approached them. "I've been looking for you," she told Etienne. "You're needed in the kitchen. You promised to make the chocolate bread pudding."

"Yeah, Dad. My mouth's ready for it, too."

Eleanor winked at Austin, then escorted her husband back to the house.

He paused in his tracks when he spotted his sister sitting on a bench alone near the gazebo.

"Jadin, you okay?"

She looked up at Austin and gave a tiny smile. "I'm fine. Just sitting here and reflecting over my life."

"I think Dad's been doing the same thing." He sat down beside her.

"From the time I was old enough to understand," Jordin began, "I knew what it meant to be a DuGrandpre. I knew about the things our grandfather went through to build this legacy he left us." Jadin looked over at him. "I have a man who loves me and I love him…only he's in Los Angeles now. His uncle owns a chain of hotels and offered him the general manager position of the one that just opened."

She glanced at Austin. "He says that he wants to marry me."

"And he wants you to move to LA."

Jadin nodded. "I love my job and I love the firm."

"More than you love this guy?"

"I don't know the answer to that question right now," she confessed.

"I know that you'll make the right decision for your life, Jadin."

"You make it sound so simple. Dad expects us to one day lead this firm. Our grandfather expected this, as well. When Aubrie announced that she wasn't going into law but becoming a chef... Austin, Aunt Rochelle and Uncle Jacques thought she'd lost her mind. Granddad almost had a stroke. He said the DuGrandpre name stood for justice. That the threats, the blood from the beating he endured, the fire and every ounce of sweat oozing from the pores of his body was for the firm. When nobody would hire him after he finished law school—he didn't quit. Granddad started his own firm. When those racists beat him, and burned down the first office, he didn't give up." Jadin paused a moment before adding, "He did all this for us so that we would have something."

"Maybe you don't have to walk out on the firm or Granddad's legacy," Austin stated. "Maybe you can have both the firm and the man you love."

"How?"

"Maybe you should do some research. Visit LA and look for office space. Put together a proposal for expanding the DuGrandpre Law Firm. Talk to Dad and Uncle Jacques about it."

"I hadn't thought of that," Jadin murmured. "Austin, this is a great idea."

"This means that you need to put together a proposal so tight it'll be difficult for them to turn down."

"I may need your help."

"I'll do what I can," he said.

* * *

"I hate that Bree had to leave so soon," Jordin said. "Did she even have a chance to sit down and eat?"

"One of her clients had some kind of setback, so she went to meet them at the hospital. We ate shortly after we got here." Austin looked around. "I haven't seen your husband. Is he here?"

She shook her head. "Ethan left this morning for business. He's going to be gone for a week. I'm trying to find ways to occupy the time while he's away." Jordin frowned. "I miss my husband already."

Austin broke into laughter. "How about Bree and I take you to dinner tomorrow after work?"

"Really?"

"Sure. I'll have her meet us at the restaurant. We can leave from here."

"You don't mind, Austin?"

"You're my sister. If you'd like, you can even stay with me while Ethan's away. Unless you like being in that huge house alone."

"His mother lives in the guesthouse, so I'll probably stay with her. I don't want to put a cramp in your routine."

"If you change your mind, just let me know."

Jordin hugged him. "I'm so glad to have you in my life, Austin. It used to hurt my feelings when I'd write to you and you never wrote me back."

"I'm sorry. I thought Dad was making you and Jadin write those letters."

"We wrote them on our own. We wanted you in our lives."

"Well, now that I'm here—I'm never going away."

Jordin smiled. "This makes me very happy."

"I'm in love with Bree," Austin announced.

His sister smiled. "Does she feel the same way about you?"

"I think so, but it's not like we've talked about it. I don't want to spook her. Besides I'm still getting used to the idea myself."

"Don't wait too long to tell Bree," Jordin advised.

Bree arrived home shortly after eight.

"Thanks for babysitting Emery. How was he?" she inquired.

"He and I had a great time. We watched a movie and he fell asleep near the end so I put him to bed in his room. That was about ten minutes ago." He sat the iPad on the coffee table.

She sat down beside him. "What are you doing?"

"Playing a video game," he responded. "Want to play?"

She dropped down beside him. "Sure."

"You are so cheating!" Bree accused when it was her turn, her laughter doing little to back up the finger she jabbed at Austin's chest.

He gently grabbed her arms. And suddenly she was tucked in the small crease between his half-sprawled form and the back of the couch.

Bree planted her palm on the center of his chest, refusing to admit how tempting it was to simply stay there, and pushed herself up.

Austin shook his head, all *who, me?* "Cheating? We're talking."

She shot him a skeptical look, not buying his wide-eyed innocent routine for one minute. That he would even try it with a mouth like his was almost too much to bear.

Reaching for her, Austin let the iPad fall to the floor.

His mouth kicked up another degree, his eyes heating in the way she'd found so startling at first, but was now beginning to look for. "Have I mentioned how sexy I find you?"

An unbidden belly flip had her glancing away before he could see how his words affected her. "I bust you for trying to cheat, and this is your response?"

"Yes."

The crook of his finger found her chin, and he pulled her back to his gaze.

"But that doesn't make what we've talked about any less true. I'm a motivated guy, set on making sure I don't let something important slip through my fingers. I want you to know what I know."

She let out an even breath, hating the way everything Austin said made sense.

Clicked, as if it was locking into some waiting place within her.

Bree was getting lost in his eyes, feeling herself drawn closer. "What I know is that you want me."

"I've got you." His voice was a low rumble against her ear. "What I want is to keep you. We're good together, Bree. It's not about glass slippers or fairy tales or love at any sight. It's about you and me fitting together. It's about this feeling of rightness. The one I've had since I met you. Tell me that you feel it, too."

"I feel it."

The connection was there. Undeniable between them.

Bree didn't want to worry about good judgment or long-term consequences. She simply wanted this man, whose promises sounded too good to be true, to deliver on the one in his eyes. "Austin," she whispered, drawing her leg slowly in, and the man with it. "You make me want…" She couldn't say it. Couldn't even think it. All her rational thought was tangled up in the rising awareness between them, the slow glide of his touch over her skin, the need simmering between them.

"I know..." he whispered. "It's the very same for me. Like I said...we fit."

"This just seems almost too good to be true," Bree said. Deep down, she was waiting for the bottom to drop out of this perfect piece of heaven she had with Austin. She wasn't a negative person—she was realistic.

Chapter 11

The following weekend Austin decided it was time to tell his mother about Emery. He was glad that Bree hadn't pressed him about coming along. He flew to Dallas that Friday after work.

"Mom..." Austin called out when he arrived.

"In here."

He followed the sound of his mother's voice to the kitchen.

Irene looked coolly over the rims of her glasses, her shrewd eyes assessing. Not a single salt-and-peppered strand of hair was out of place, curled back from her temples stylishly and stopping just below her collar. "Nice of you to come visit."

"Mom, I would've come a lot sooner, but I've had a lot going on. Besides, the last time I came home, you were still upset with me for leaving." No one could hold a grudge better than Irene DuGrandpre, Austin thought to himself.

She didn't respond.

"I guess you're still mad."

"I'm not mad. Just *hurt*." She paused a moment before

asking, "How could you choose that *man* over me? I was the one who sacrificed everything for you."

"I didn't *choose* him, Mom. He's my father and I wanted to get to know him for myself. All my life I've heard your version of what happened—I wanted to hear his side, too."

"Oh, so you think I've been lying to you. The man cheated on me throughout our marriage."

"I never said you lied about anything."

"Then what does it matter—he's only gonna tell you something to try and make me look bad."

"He didn't do that, Mom. He accepted his part in what happened. He owned up to being unfaithful."

She rolled her eyes. "How cavalier…"

"When are you going to stop being so angry with him? I'm a grown man."

"Maybe a few years after I'm dead… I might be able to forgive him then." She gave Austin a tiny smile.

He embraced her. "I love you, Mom. Nothing or no one can ever change that."

"So how is Etienne?"

"He's doing well," Austin responded. "Jordin recently got married. She wanted to invite you to the wedding, but I told her that it wasn't a good idea."

"You right about that," Irene uttered. "I'm happy for her, though. I'll send a gift back with you."

"Mom, she and Jadin really want to meet you."

"Why?"

"Because you're my mother and they consider you an extended member of the family. Regardless of how you may feel—you are still a DuGrandpre."

Irene made a face. "Humph. My mama and my daddy's girlfriend used to cook together whenever they came to visit, but I'ma tell you now. I'm not the one for that kinda mess."

Austin laughed. "No one expects you and Eleanor to be anything other than cordial, I'm sure."

"I'm just saying…"

"Dad wants to reach out to you. He wants to apologize."

Irene shook her head. "Tell him to save it for the Lord. I don't want to hear anything that man has to say. The time for it was a long time ago."

"You still love him," Austin said.

"Boy, you've lost your last mind," she declared.

"You divorced my father twenty-seven years ago. If there weren't feelings involved—it wouldn't bother you so much after all that time. Then the fact that you've never remarried, although three different men proposed to you over the years…you still love my dad."

"I never remarried because those guys were fine to date, but they…" Her voice died and Irene released a long sigh. "Son, the truth is that I just couldn't bear getting my heart broke a second time."

She walked over to the breakfast table and sat down. Austin joined her.

"I met your father when I was in the ninth grade. I thought he and Jacques were the cutest boys in school, but Etienne, there was something special about him. He could just smile and I would melt. He was my first love."

His mother had never discussed her relationship with his father before. The only thing Austin knew about his parents was that his mother had gotten pregnant in college and they married. That child died and a few months later, she was pregnant again with him.

"When we lost that first baby," Irene was saying, "Etienne changed. He was happy when we found out that we were having you, but things between us was different. He had just gotten accepted into law school and I graduated from nursing school…" She shook her head. "Things just

changed. At first, I thought it was because we were both
in school and spent most of our time focused on finishing college. A lot of people thought we wouldn't graduate
because we were going to have a child. Your grandfather, especially. I don't think that man ever liked me. He
didn't think I was good enough to wear the DuGrandpre
name. That's why I never went back to my maiden name.
To spite him."

"When did you find out Dad was cheating on you?"
Austin inquired.

"The day you were born," Irene responded. "He was
nowhere to be found when I went into labor. And when he
finally showed up, I could smell liquor and the woman's
perfume on him."

"Yet you stayed."

"I didn't leave your father, but I never let him touch
me after that. After I had saved up some money and had
worked at the hospital for a year, then I decided it was time
for me to go. I wanted to make sure I had some security."

"Dad said when he found out that you were in labor, it
scared him. He remembered all you'd gone through with
my brother, only for him to be stillborn. He went to a bar
and got drunk. A woman came on to him and..."

"I know what happened after that."

"He said nothing happened, but that you would never
believe him," Austin stated. "The affairs started after that
and I believe him. He felt he'd already lost you and he
didn't want to be alone."

"Etienne wasn't there when I needed him the most. I
was scared, too." A tear slid down Irene's cheek. "We'd
both lost a child. He should've been there for me."

Austin reached over and covered his mother's hand
with his own. "He realizes this now. Mom, he truly regrets
what happened and this is why he wants to talk to you."

Irene removed her glasses and wiped her eyes. "What's done can't be undone. Regardless of any apology, Etienne can't unbreak my heart."

"I'm sorry he hurt you."

She touched his cheek. "You have nothing to be sorry about, Austin. I know that a boy needs his father and I kept you away from Etienne. It was wrong, but I wanted to hurt him for the pain and humiliation he caused me. I'm the one who owes you an apology. Baby, I'm so sorry."

Austin smiled. "I don't think I turned out so bad. You did a good job."

"I'm so proud of you, son."

Irene pushed away from the table and rose to her feet. "I need to get started on dinner."

"Why don't we go out?" he suggested. "My treat."

She shook her head. "There's no way my son is gonna eat somebody else's cooking on his first night home. I'm making your favorite. Barbecue chicken."

After dinner Austin helped his mother clean the kitchen. They settled in the family room to watch television thirty minutes later.

"Mom, I need to tell you something."

"What is it, son?"

"Getting to know my dad wasn't the only reason I moved to Charleston. To be honest, I didn't go there to seek him out at all."

"Then why?" Displeasure was written all over her face. "Please tell me that you didn't go chasing after that Jasmine. Boy, I told you that girl isn't the right woman for you."

"When Jasmine left town, she was pregnant."

Irene gave Austin a sidelong glance. "What's that got to do with you?"

"She was carrying my child, Mom."

"You sure about that?"

Austin nodded. "I found out the woman who adopted him lived in Charleston—that's why I moved there."

"Does Etienne know about this?"

"No, I wanted to tell you first."

"I never liked Jasmine and before you do anything—you need to have a paternity test. I wouldn't trust anything that girl says."

"She didn't tell me. I spoke with Cheryl."

"I'm not so sure you can trust her, either. Why did she wait so long to share this information with you?"

"She was pregnant and said she couldn't face me without telling me the truth of what happened."

"I heard she and Jasmine fell out. That's why Cheryl came back to Dallas. As far as I'm concerned, this is all suspect."

"I believe her, Mom."

"Well, what are you gonna do?"

"I intend to get my son. I never agreed to an adoption and I didn't terminate my parental rights."

"Then just have the adoption nullified."

"It's not that simple, Mom."

She looked at him. "Why not? You're a lawyer."

The woman who adopted Emery is actually a friend of Jordin's. I've been getting to know her."

Irene frowned. "Know her how?"

"I'm dating her, Mom."

"Do you think this is a good idea, son? What happens if you two don't work out? What then?"

"Emery will be my son regardless of my relationship with Bree."

Irene shook her head. "I hope you know what you're doing."

"Emery loves Bree," he responded. "She's a good

mother and I really care for her. If you want to know the
truth, I think it's the perfect solution for us."

"Then why haven't you told her the truth?"

While his mother was at work, Austin decided to have
lunch at one of his favorite Dallas restaurants.

While he waited for his food to arrive, he made a call.
"Hey, sweetheart."

"How are things going with you and your mom?" Bree
asked.

"Great. She was a little stiff when I first arrived, but
she's fine now. We sat down and had a really good talk
yesterday."

"I'm sorry I missed your call last night. After I got
Emery settled in bed, I took a shower and fell out."

"I called you because I was missing that sweet voice
of yours."

"I miss you. It's a bit strange to not see you every day.
I think I've gotten a bit spoiled."

Austin chuckled. "Don't worry, I'll be back in a couple of days."

He paid the check and left.

"Austin…"

He turned around to the sound of a familiar voice.
Jasmine Reynolds.

"I heard that you left town." She looked around as if
suddenly anxious to escape his presence.

"Is that why you're here?" he asked. "Because you
didn't think you'd run into me."

Awkwardly, she cleared her throat, arms folded across
her chest. "Why would I worry about *that*?"

"Because I know about Emery."

Her smile disappeared. "Cheryl told you. I wish that
witch would mind her own business."

"*You* should've told me that you were pregnant."

"Why? Nothing would've changed between us, Austin. You didn't want to marry me."

"So, you leave town with my child to punish me?"

"I left to raise my son alone. I needed to start over someplace fresh."

"*Raise him,*" he uttered. "You gave him up for adoption."

Jasmine looked as if she was searching for a plausible answer. "Once I had the baby, I realized that I couldn't handle being a mother. I tried reaching out to you, but you'd changed your number and I didn't know where you were," she responded. "I placed an ad in the newspaper."

He knew she was lying. "*You expect me to believe that?* This was all intentional. I'm not even named on the birth certificate as his father."

"How do you know that?"

"I have a copy." Austin glanced down at the wedding ring on her finger. "You finally got the husband you wanted—at Cheryl's expense."

"I knew she was in her feelings, but I can't believe Cheryl would betray me like this."

"Are you really going to pull the betrayal card? You married the man she was dating."

Jasmine shrugged. "It's not my fault she couldn't keep him."

Shaking his head, he stated, "You're something else."

"Austin, I don't know what you're planning, but listen to me…you really don't want to pursue this. Cheryl never should've gotten you involved."

"This is my son. Do you really think I'm going to just sit back and do nothing?"

Jasmine looked him straight in the eye. "I don't see where you have much choice, Austin. I hate that things went bad between us because I really loved you. If you want to know the truth… I still love you."

He shook his head. "You don't do what you did and claim to love someone."

"Sometimes you have to make hard choices—this was probably the hardest one I've ever had to make, but I felt it was for the best. I hope that one day you'll be able to forgive me."

"Hardly," he uttered. "Do you ever think about him?"

She glanced down at her watch. "I have to pick up my mother, but I'd like to finish this conversation, Austin. Can you meet me for dinner tonight?"

"How will your husband feel about it?"

"He's in Los Angeles in the studio all week. I married a record producer."

"Sounds like your type."

Jasmine's jaw tightened. "I guess I deserve that. Austin, I know that you think I'm a terrible person, but I did what was best for Emery. Please, Austin…have dinner with me. We need to talk and I promise I'll tell you everything. I owe you the truth."

"What time?"

"Six o'clock. Meet me at Copeland's. It used to be our favorite spot." Jasmine pulled out a piece of paper and wrote on it. "Here's my number. In case you change your mind."

"What's wrong, son?"

"I just ran into Jasmine."

"*What?* Has she moved back to Dallas? If so, I'm so glad that you live in Charleston now."

"I didn't ask, but I guess she's here visiting family. I never expected to see her again, especially not so soon."

"What happened?"

"She said that she didn't tell me about the pregnancy because it wouldn't have changed my mind about marriage. She wants to have dinner with me tonight to discuss everything."

"I heard she got married, but I don't know if it's true."

"She had on a wedding ring," Austin responded. "She told she married a record producer."

"Is her husband here with her?"

"No, ma'am."

"Then you better stay home with me. That girl just trying to get you someplace and seduce you. Boy, you don't need that kind of trouble."

Austin wasn't sure what Jasmine was plotting, but he thought it better to listen to his mother and stay as far away from the woman as possible.

He picked up his cell phone to call her, then changed his mind. He didn't want her to have his number, so he called from the landline.

When she answered, Austin went straight to the purpose of his call. "Jasmine, I don't think it's a good idea for us to have dinner."

"Is this how you really feel or how your mother feels?"

"Why do you always have to go there?" he asked. "Leave my mom out of this."

"Miss Irene never liked me. I believe that's why you didn't want to marry me."

"You're wrong," Austin stated. "We weren't getting along, Jasmine, and things were not getting any better. That's why I didn't want to get married. I didn't want to end up in divorce court."

"Austin, I really want to sit down and talk to you face-to-face. I know Cheryl's probably told you a bunch of mess. She—"

He cut her off by interjecting, "She only told me about Emery. I didn't want to know or hear about anything else."

"How can you be so cold to me? Austin, we were together for over three years."

"I know that."

"So, you have no feelings for me whatsoever? They just vanished with the wind?"

"Jasmine, you're married or so you say. You've moved on and I wish you all the happiness you can muster. What I feel or don't feel shouldn't matter."

"It does to me," she insisted.

"The only thing we have to discuss is Emery."

"Austin, I wasn't ready to be a mother. I thought I could do it, but after he was born—I realized that I wasn't Mommy material."

"So why didn't you just bring him to me? You have to know that I would've taken my son."

"I was still angry with you. I was hurt and I acted out of that hurt. If I could do things differently, I would, Austin."

He didn't respond.

"He is with a good family and he's happy."

"How do you know?" Austin asked. "Do you even know where he is?"

"He's in Vegas."

He didn't bother to tell her otherwise. From the sound of it, Jasmine wasn't interested in her son. As much as it grieved him, she had done the right thing by terminating her parental rights. Emery was with a mother who adored him. He deserved someone like Bree.

"I hope you don't hate me."

"I don't," he responded.

"Austin…"

"I have to go," he stated. "Goodbye, Jasmine."

Chapter 12

"How was your trip?" Jordin asked. "And your mother? I'm sure she was thrilled to see you."

"It was interesting," Austin responded. "My mom and I had a good time together. I have a wedding gift in my car for you—it's from her."

"Oh, that's so sweet." Jordin sat down in one of the visitor chairs. "What made your trip interesting? I got the feeling that it didn't have to do with your mother."

"Jasmine was in town. She's Emery's biological mother."

"And your ex-girlfriend."

Austin nodded. "I was not prepared to see her."

"How did it go?"

"She claims that she didn't tell me about the pregnancy because she knew I didn't want to marry her. Jasmine invited me to have dinner with her that evening to discuss it further. She said she owed me the truth."

"Did you have dinner with her?"

Austin shook his head. "There wasn't much else she could tell me. Nothing she would've said could change this mess she caused. She lied to the courts and gave up her son for marriage to some record producer. I guess it was a pretty good trade-off."

Jordin shook her head. "How did you ever get involved with someone so heartless?"

"I didn't see her true colors until much later."

"You didn't tell her that you found Emery?"

"No, there's no way I would do that—I don't trust Jasmine at all."

"Do you still love her?"

"No. Those feelings went away long before I knew about Emery. She and I were toxic. That's why I ended the relationship."

"If you'd known about the baby, do you think you would've made the same decision? To break up with her?"

"I honestly don't know. I never would've abandoned my son. I do know that Jasmine and I never would've gotten married, but I would be in Emery's life."

"So, what happens now between you and Bree?"

"I don't want to hurt her, Jordin. Like you said, she's an innocent party to this drama. Things are good between us. I won't just snatch Emery from her. She's his mother. I want what's best for him, and right now that's Bree."

"He loves her."

"I know," Austin said. "I see the way his eyes light up whenever he looks at her. It's the same for Bree and she's good to him."

"I can see how much this hurts you," Jordin said. "I can see how much you love your son. Trust me when I tell you that this will work itself out. Look at Ryker and Garland. Their daughters were switched at birth and now they are one happy family."

"I like Bree, but I can't say we're heading toward marriage. Not yet."

"I hear the two of you are spending a lot of time together. I'd say it's a little more than just *like*."

Austin broke into a grin. "I enjoy her company and I
admit, I'm very attracted to her."

"Don't play with her heart."

"I wouldn't do that," he assured Jordin.

"I'm holding you to that. Bree is my best friend and I
don't want to see her hurt. When she finds out that you're
Emery's birth father—I'm not sure what it will do to her,
but knowing that you don't intend to rip him out of her
arms will help."

Austin enjoyed spending time with Bree and Emery.
Some evenings they would order out for dinner or settle in
with grilled cheese sandwiches. A few times he'd brought
work from the office and while she stretched out on the
sofa reading some psychological journal, he would stretch
out on the floor with his laptop.

Regardless of what they were doing, Austin was
acutely aware of her every movement. Bree felt comfortable around him and he felt comfortable around her. She
had allowed him into her space and he had allowed her
into his. He'd never shared this kind of closeness with any
woman—not even Jasmine. At one point Austin figured
he never would, but Bree had proved him wrong.

Just as he rang the doorbell, he heard Emery crying.

Bree opened the door.

Austin halted abruptly at the sight of her holding a sobbing Emery in her arms. His throat constricted at the picture they made. The sight of Bree and his son together
did something to his heart he knew he'd never get back.

He instinctively reached for Emery. "What's wrong,
buddy?"

"I got a boo-boo…"

"He fell halfway down the stairs," Bree explained. "He has a little bruise, but he's okay." She touched his arm. "I'm glad you're back. We missed you."

Austin broke into a grin. "Really? Can't live without me, huh."

"Naw…" she uttered. "I just said that to make you feel good. I didn't think about you at all."

He laughed. "Good, 'cause I didn't miss you, either." Austin felt his pulse take off at just the sight of her. She was wearing jeans and a pale pink sleeveless top. Her dark brown hair was pulled back in a ponytail.

He calmed Emery enough to put him down, then followed Bree into the kitchen. "What are you making?" he asked, watching her drop a stick of butter into a skillet on the stove, Next, she begin chopping cloves of garlic.

"Shrimp scampi."

Bree swept the chopped garlic into the melted butter, the scent wafting through the kitchen and making his stomach growl. She turned back to the stove, slid several dozen fresh deveined shrimp into the skillet with the butter and garlic, then began to chop some scallions with a cleaver.

It wasn't long before they sat down to eat.

As the hour drew later, Austin offered to give Emery his bath.

"Thanks, I appreciate it," Bree said. "I could use a few minutes to make a couple of phone calls."

After he climbed into bed, Emery handed Austin a book that was already well-read, the pages opening easily to the beginning. "I want to hear this one."

He was curled beside him, holding tight to a blanket and his Thor figurine.

"Yes, if you do not know my face, you will know me by my deeds. I am Loki…" Austin read.

"He Thor's brotha," Emery uttered. "Bad man."

Smiling, he read on, loving the sound of his giggles.

Austin finished one book and was handed another by Emery. *"Goodnight Moon,"* he muttered.

"This is the last one for tonight, okay?"

The little boy yawned.

Austin's eyelids grew heavy as a yawn overtook him. Emery cuddled against him. "I happy you here."

"Me, too." He stifled another yawn. "I don't want to be anyplace else."

Bree hovered in the doorway, her gaze on Austin and Emery as they slept. She wavered with indecision on waking him. She pulled out her phone and snapped a photo of the two, then eased out of the room.

She went to her office and uploaded the photo to her computer.

He looks so handsome, she thought. *They look like they are truly father and son.* No man had ever shown this much interest in her child, but then she hadn't given any a real chance to do so. Austin was different, this much she did know. He was unlike any man she'd ever met, and this list included her late husband, Caleb.

Things were great between her and Austin. The more time she spent with him, the more her body yearned for him. Bree was ready to take their relationship to the next level. Austin had been wonderful by waiting until she was ready.

Her eyes traveled to the picture on the screen. *Austin, I'm ready.*

She heard a sound and looked up.

"Hey, sorry about that," Austin said as he entered her office. "I didn't mean to fall asleep like that. I guess I'm more exhausted than I thought."

Bree turned off the monitor, got up from the desk and walked toward him. "It's no problem."

"It's late, so I'll get out of here."

She stood as close to him as she could get. "You don't have to leave, Austin."

He met her gaze. "What are you saying?"

"I *want* you to stay," Bree responded. "You can sleep in my room."

"Are you sure about this?"

"Yes." His steady gaze bored in her in silent expectation.

In response, she led him by the hand to her bedroom.

He took her mouth as if it was his to do with as he pleased.

Bree's fingers curled into his shirt; her moan sliding free of her mouth and into his, awakening feelings that had lain dormant for a while.

Hot desire.

Explosive.

Consuming and intense.

Standing in the middle of the floor, they undressed each other in silence.

His arms slid around her waist, pulling her in tight. "I knew you were special from the first time I ever saw you. The reason I'm telling you this is because I want you to know where you stand with me before we become intimate. I'm not looking for casual sex. I want something more."

Bree was moved by his words. "I feel the same way."

She watched the play of emotions on his face. Bree lifted her arms, linking them around his neck, holding Austin to her.

His arms tightened until she could hardly draw breath.

"I need you," he whispered, dropping his mouth to the line of her jaw, nibbling at her throat.

Austin swept her, weightless, into his arms and carried her to the bed. After placing her in the middle of the bed, he crawled in behind her.

Bree could feel his uneven breathing on her cheek as he held her close. The touch of his hand was almost unbearable in its tenderness. His mouth covered hers hungrily, leaving her mouth burning with fire.

The touch of her lips on his sent a shock wave through Austin's entire body with a savage intensity. As he roused her passion, his own need grew stronger.

Passion pounded the blood through her heart, chest and head, causing Bree to breathe in deep, soul-drenching drafts.

Holding her close, Austin rolled her across the bed and she went with him willingly, eagerly, entangling her legs with his.

Heartbeats thundered and each breath was a sigh sifting into the quiet. All that existed was the slide of skin on skin, the soft sighs of their heightened breathing, the crashing beats of their hearts.

Later, Bree watched the rise and fall of Austin's chest as he slept, thinking about what had transpired earlier. He made her feel loved in the way that he touched her, kissed her and held her in his arms.

Austin placed a protective arm around her, pulling her closer to him. He never opened his eyes.

When he was sleeping soundly, Bree eased out of bed and padded barefoot to the bathroom to shower.

Afterward, she slipped on her robe and went to check on Emery.

The little boy was asleep, his Iron Man toy in his hands. A smile trembled on Bree's lips as she watched him, her heart full of love. The hair on the back of her neck stood up.

She glanced over her shoulder to find Austin standing in the doorway. He must have awakened and found her gone.

He didn't enter, but his gaze was trained on Emery.

No words passed between them as they lovingly watched over the little boy.

Together, they returned to her bedroom.

The next morning Austin slid out of the bed, careful not to make a sound. He tucked the blanket higher around Bree's sleeping form. It was nearly dawn, and the temperature was cool in the bedroom.

He couldn't sleep.

There was too much on his mind. He felt a thread of guilt at the thought of keeping secrets from the woman he was in love with. *There shouldn't be any secrets between us.*

He stretched and yawned.

She mumbled something in her sleep, but didn't open her eyes.

He pulled her closer to him.

Austin never considered that he would fall in love with Bree. His focus had been to right the wrong that had been done to him. But getting to know her changed everything. He found in her a kinship. Before long she had stolen his heart and now here they were—it was time for him to come forward.

No more secrets.

Chapter 13

Bree came downstairs dressed in a pair of denim shorts and a tank top. When she reached the kitchen, Austin already had a skillet on the burner and was half-buried in the refrigerator, pulling out ingredients.

"I wondered where you were," she said.

He closed the door, put a carton of eggs on the counter and turned to face her. "Good morning, gorgeous." Austin kissed her. "Any regrets?"

She lifted her chin, squared her shoulders and looked him dead in the eye. "None." Her body was still humming, buzzing with sensation. "What are you making?" she asked.

"Spinach and mushroom omelets, bacon and toast."

"Can I help?"

He cracked eggs into a bowl and handed her a whisk while he put butter in the pan. "Here you go."

Minutes later Emery ran into the kitchen. "Hey, Mommy...hey, Au'tin."

"Good morning, sweetie," she responded before bending down to plant a kiss on his forehead.

He climbed onto a chair at the counter. Propped on his knees, he asked, "What you makin'?"

"Austin's making us a special breakfast. Isn't that nice?"

Emery nodded. "I happy."

"Me, too, buddy," Austin murmured. "I'm happy, too."

Bree took a seat at the counter while Austin moved around her kitchen as though he'd spent time in it before. Humming softly, Austin opened cabinets, pulling out the ingredients he needed for his meal.

After breakfast, they took Emery to the park.

Austin wanted to talk to Bree, but didn't want to distract her from keeping an eye on Emery. Maybe it was too soon to tell her, especially after making love to her the night before. She looked so happy and he didn't want to ruin that happiness.

"You look like you're in deep thought," Bree said.

"I was thinking about you."

She inclined her head. "What about me?"

"Just in the short time I've known you... Bree, you make me feel in a way no other woman has made me feel. You're incredible."

She smiled.

"The last thing I've ever wanted to do is hurt you."

Bree's eyes traveled to where Emery was playing and stayed. "I'm not worried about you hurting me, Austin. It's strange because I don't trust easy, but with you—I don't have any doubts in my heart."

Her words should've touched him, but instead he was filled with guilt.

She reached over, placing her hand in his. "The way you treat Emery—it's as if he were your own flesh and blood. My son adores you, Austin. He's never taken to anyone the way he took to you. I pride myself on being a good judge of character, so I know that you're a good man."

"I hope you'll always feel this way," he uttered.

Bree gave his hand a gentle squeeze. "I'm sure I will."

A couple of days later, Bree met Jordin at Indulgence, their favorite locale for spa dates.

"I'm so glad you booked this appointment because I really need a massage." Jordin sank down in one of the chairs in the reception area. "This was a crazy week for me. I'm so glad it's the weekend."

Bree pulled the folds of her plush robe together. "I needed a girls' day."

"You're tired of my brother already?"

She laughed. "No, not at all. I just miss hanging out with you and Jadin. I didn't know she was going to Los Angeles or I would've picked another date."

"She and Michael are trying to sort out their relationship."

"Long-distance relationships are a challenge," Bree stated. "It could work if they both put in the effort, which it looks like they're doing."

Jordin took a long sip of her mimosa. "My brother is in love with that little boy of yours."

"I know. You should see them together. Austin gets down on the floor with him, and it's like he and Emery are the only two people in the world. He is going to be a great father."

"Are you thinking about him as Emery's dad?"

Bree smiled. "I'd like that. Austin and I are in a really good space. We love each other, and we're both looking to settle down. I think there's a possibility that we might seriously consider marriage."

"I think it's more than a possibility," Jordin said. "You both want the same thing and that is a family."

It was past one o'clock when Austin knocked on Jordin's door. "Busy?"

She shook her head. "Come in."

He swung the door closed and took a seat on the chair in her office. "I'm going to ask Bree to marry me."

"Wow...that's great," she murmured. "When?"

"I was thinking about tonight, but before that I'm going to tell her everything."

"I'm glad."

"She's a good mother to Emery."

"I told you that there wasn't anything to worry about with Bree."

"You were right. She's the kind of mother I would want for my son. As much as I hate what Jasmine did, I'm glad Emery has Bree. I can tell he adores her."

"How do you think she's going to react to finding out that you're Emery's father?"

"I wish I knew," Austin muttered. "I hope she'll understand the toll this has taken on me. My child was stolen away from me before I ever knew he existed. I intend on being in his life and I was willing to do whatever I had to do to make that happen."

"But then you met Bree..."

He smiled. "I love her. The three of us belong together. The first time we went out with Emery—it felt so right. This is the way it's supposed to be. We are a family. I want to make it official by marrying her—we will raise Emery together."

"I would still advise that you petition the court for paternity and have his birth certificate amended with your name as his father."

"I intend to do that. I want his last name changed to DuGrandpre."

"As it should be."

Chapter 14

"Is Austin in his office?" Bree inquired.

"I think so, Dr. Collins. Do you want me to call him or do you want to just go back there?"

"I need to see Jordin, too, so I can just walk to the back."

Bree decided to go by Jordin's office first. As she neared, she could hear Austin talking and smiled.

What are those two up to?

Just as she was about to open the door, Jordin's words stopped her.

"How do you think she's going to react to finding out that you're Emery's father?"

"I wish I knew," she heard Austin say. "I hope she'll understand the toll this has taken on me. My child was stolen away from me before I ever knew he existed. I intend on being in his life and I was willing to do whatever I had to do to make that happen."

Bree shuddered as shock penetrated her core.

Austin... Emery's father?

She glanced around, hoping no one was paying attention to her. Bree backed away from the door, turned and walked briskly toward the elevator. She couldn't see Jordin or Austin right now.

His words, "I intend on being in his life and I was willing to do whatever I had to do to make that happen," played over and over in her mind.

He had been using her to get to Emery.

Tears filled her eyes and spilled down her cheeks.

Bree wiped her face with the backs of her hands as she made her way to her car.

I can't break down now. I need to think.

Austin wanted to take her child from her and she wasn't about to let that happen.

I can't lose my baby.

Bree drove straight to the preschool to pick up Emery.

Once home, she immediately started packing. "I'm not going to let him take you from me," she whispered as she packed a suitcase.

"Where we going?" Emery asked. "Au'tin coming with us?"

"No, baby, he's not going to be able to come. It's just going to be you and Mommy."

"Why you cryin'? You got a ouchy?"

Bree thought of her broken heart. "Mommy has a big ouchy."

Emery gave her a hug. "You feel better now?"

She nodded. "Thank you, baby."

An hour later Bree stopped by her neighbor's house to let her know that she and Emery would be away for about a week. In truth, she wasn't sure how long they would be gone, but she didn't want to worry her friend.

In the car, she tried to put the pieces together. Now she could understand why Austin was so enamored with Emery. Jordin knew this and aided her brother in getting to know Bree. She had never felt so betrayed in her life.

Bree prided herself on being a good judge of character, but she had been completely off the mark where Jordin and Austin were concerned. It would be a while before they realized that she and Emery were gone. By the time they found out—they would be long gone.

Austin picked up the phone to call Bree. He'd made reservations for them at High Cotton. When she didn't answer, he left her a message with the time he would be picking her up.

He pulled a box out of the small shopping bag. He'd spent his lunch hour looking for the perfect engagement ring and he'd found it. Austin couldn't wait for Bree to see it.

An hour passed.

Austin checked his phone. It wasn't like Bree to not return his call. If she was busy, she normally sent a text letting him know when she would be able to talk. He assumed it must be a busy day for her.

He didn't call her again until right before he left the office for the day. Austin hadn't heard from her, so he decided to go by her office.

When he arrived, it was completely dark.

Austin called her.

No answer.

His gut instincts told him something wasn't quite right, but he couldn't figure out what had gone wrong.

Austin drove over to her house.

When he knocked, there was no answer.

Sara opened her door. "Hey, Austin," she greeted. "Sugar, they're not there. She and Emery are on vacation. I'm surprised she didn't mention it. They left today."

"No, she didn't tell me," he muttered. "Are you sure?"

"That's what she told me. She said they would be gone for a week."

"Did she tell you where they were going?"

Sara shook her head. "Naw, she didn't, which is kinda odd. She usually good about letting me know where she's going. Bree was in a hurry and she looked upset. I called her about an hour ago to check on her, but she didn't answer."

Austin spent the next hour pacing the floor, trying to understand what had happened with Bree. They got along well and thus far, their relationship was amazing. With every minute they spent together, Austin fell more in love with her. And she loved him. He was certain of that.

Why didn't she tell me she was leaving town?

A sick churning started in the pit of his stomach. Spinning around, Austin went to the living room and picked up the phone.

He tried calling Bree once again.

No answer.

Maybe she was on a plane. This would explain why she hadn't returned his or Sara's phone calls. Still, they had prearranged plans to have dinner this evening. Bree never once mentioned that she would be going away. This was something that had come about quickly.

Austin sat in the darkened living room staring out the window and watching the occasional sweep of car lights beam in from the street.

The refrigerator kicked on. The ice maker dumped.

He rubbed a hand over his chest.

It hurt.

Bree's thoughts were jagged and painful as she turned on the dusty road that led to her grandmother's house in

Roseville, Georgia. A heaviness centered in her chest as she felt an inexplicable feeling of heartbreak.

Emery was in the backseat sleeping. He had been no trouble during the four-hour drive from Charleston. She was so proud of him.

Tears filled Bree's eyes at the idea of losing her son. *I love him so much. I can't lose my baby.* Worse, she couldn't believe that Jordin had participated in something like this—they had been close friends since college.

How could she do this to me?

She refused to spend any time thinking about Austin. He could've been honest with her—he didn't have to try to manipulate her. Bree was hurt and furious with him.

The first thing she had to do in the morning after she got Emery settled was to call her attorney. She needed to make sure the adoption was legal. After all, Austin wasn't listed on the birth certificate. She didn't want to lose her son. He was her everything.

Bree looked at her phone.

She had messages from both Sara and Austin. She wasn't in the mood to talk to anyone tonight. All Bree wanted to do was take a bath and go to bed, but she didn't want to worry her neighbor, so she sent her a text.

Hey, I'm okay. Just needed some time to think. Will explain everything when I return.
Bree

After her bath, she saw a text from Sara.

Austin came by. He didn't know you were leaving. Everything OK with you two?

Bree decided to be honest.

No. He is part of the reason I left. We'll talk when I get back.

There was another call from Austin.
Emery was still sleeping, so she joined him in the bed. Bree didn't want to spend a moment away from him.

Chapter 15

Coming to Roseville had always given Bree a sense of peace. It had come as a surprise when her foster parents received a letter from a pastor, informing them that her grandmother has left the house to Bree.

She was in college at the time and traveled to Georgia to meet with the Reverend Moore. He had been using the house for visiting pastors to stay. The church had been paying the expenses of the taxes and utilities for the place since the death of her grandmother.

Bree allowed the church to continue using the house. When the Reverend Moore passed away, the congregation dwindled down until the doors closed for good. She decided to renovate the house and keep it as a place for her and Emery to come and relax.

She loved the way the flowers bloomed all around the porch in summer and how the trees shifted from green to a golden spectrum of orange and red in the fall. It rained around midnight, the raindrops falling in a monotonous drone that lulled her to sleep.

Today, though, she felt restless.

Even the November air seemed to be holding its breath,

waiting for something. She felt that same sense of anticipation inside her like the flutter of butterfly wings. Something was about to happen.

Bree tried to go back to her book, but her mind kept
wandering. She found herself looking down the long dirt
road. If anyone had been coming, she would have been
able to see the dust cloud miles away.

Nothing moved.

The weather was still warm, despite the cloud casting
a dark, cool shadow.

Bree shivered, sensing a change in the air.

Austin burst into his sister's office without knocking.
"Have you talked to Bree?"

Jordin shook her head. "I left her a message earlier, but
she hasn't called me back. Did you try her office?"

"She's not there," Austin responded. "Her neighbor said
that Bree told her that she and Emery were going to be
gone for a week. On vacation. The thing is that she never
mentioned going anywhere to me and she's not returning
my calls or texts. I think she's run away for some reason."

Frowning, Jordin asked, "Why would she do that?"

He shrugged. "Something's up with Bree. I just don't
know what it is."

Jordin picked up the phone. "This isn't making any
sense. Let me try again to see if I can reach her."

Austin sank down in one of the chairs facing her.

"Hey, it's me. Austin and I are getting worried about
you. Can you give us a call or send a text just to let us
know you're okay? *Please* let us hear from you."

"I don't have a good feeling about this," Austin said.
"Do you think she found out that I was Emery's father
somehow?"

"I don't see how she could, but it's the only thing that

makes sense. I know Bree and she wouldn't just take off like this. She certainly wouldn't just avoid phone calls. It's not like her."

"Any idea where she might go?"

"Not really."

"Do you think she'd go back to Vegas?"

Jordin shook her head. "No, she didn't really like living out there."

Her cell phone vibrated.

She picked it up. "Bree just sent a text."

Jordin read it aloud.

"I am fine. I know about Emery and I'm not going to lose my son. I will do whatever I have to do to keep him. Bree."

She looked up at Austin. "I don't know how she found out."

"It doesn't matter now. The only thing I care about is finding Emery and Bree. I can't lose either of them."

"Now that I think about it," Jordin said, "her grandmother left her house to Bree. She used to let a church use it, and she fixed it up. I know it's in Georgia, but I don't remember the name of the town. It's near Atlanta, though."

Austin rose to his feet. "We can search for a deed or tax record."

"She didn't call because she knows that I kept the truth from her, as well," Jordin stated. "Bree's angry with me."

"Once I get a chance to talk to her, I'll fix all of this, sis," he assured her. "I'm not going to let you take the fall for my actions."

"I was the one who told you to wait before telling her the truth."

"Neither of us had any idea that Bree and I would get involved. I should've told her the truth."

"What are you going to do now?"

Austin headed to the door. "I'm going to find out where they are and bring them home. I love Bree and I'm going to tell her that I want a life with her and Emery."

"I hope that we haven't lost all of Bree's trust."

"I'll do whatever I have to do to get it back," he vowed. If he'd listened to his common sense, none of this would have happened. Austin drew in a deep breath and let it out slowly. All the common sense in the world wouldn't change how he'd handled this situation.

He loved Bree. Being with her energized him and gave him hope for a better future. She was the other half of his heart. Giving her up without a fight was out of the question.

Bree stared at the text she'd sent Jordin and silently debated if she'd done the right thing. She had grown tired of all the phone calls and the messages. Despite her anger with Jordin, she didn't want her to worry.

Turning the phone off, she slid it back into the pocket of her jeans.

Her heart broke all over again each time she thought of the man she had come to love. When she lost Caleb, Bree never considered she would ever fall in love again.

But Austin was only using her to get to Emery.

She tried to swallow the lump that lingered in her throat. Bree wasn't sure she could ever forgive him.

If he is truly Emery's father—he deserves to be a part of the boy's life.

She thought back to what she'd overheard of Austin's conversation with Jordin. He hadn't known about the child until after the adoption. If this was true, then why didn't he just tell her the truth? Why all the secrecy?

Bree had a lot of questions, but she wasn't ready to talk to Austin. Her attorney hadn't called her back. She needed to be prepared legally before she sat down to discuss anything with him, so until then—Bree intended to avoid Austin.

She went to check on Emery.

He lay on top of the covers fast asleep.

She left the door open a crack.

Two steps down the hall, Bree turned back for another look. Emery hadn't stirred. Fingers crossed that he stayed that way, she went into his room and sat cross-legged on the floor, putting a puzzle back together.

The truth was that she couldn't stay in Georgia forever. She still had a practice and clients who depended on her. She would have to go back to Charleston.

Or did she?

Bree glanced around the house. With more renovations, she could make it a perfect home for her and Emery.

But what if I lose him?

Emotionally drained and her eyes heavy with fatigue, she made her way to her bedroom.

Completely dressed, Bree lay down on top of the comforter, turning on her side. She was too confused and exhausted to think about the possibility.

Her heart couldn't handle the pain.

Chapter 16

Austin turned up the radio to drown out the thunder exploding around him. It had been nice weather when he left Charleston; once he crossed the Georgia line, it was pouring down rain. He had never enjoyed driving in bad weather conditions and was anxious to get to his destination.

Bakeries, a couple of inns, restaurants and shops lined the main street of Roseville, Georgia. He had never heard of the small town located thirty miles outside Atlanta. According to the welcome sign at the entrance of Roseville, there were about ten thousand residents.

His windshield wipers fought valiantly in a losing battle to maintain visibility. It was almost 9:30 p.m. The streetlights did very little to help. Austin continued driving, heading toward a rural section of town. The lane was long and straight, and unpaved. His tires would be covered in mud, he knew. He had never been a fan of rain.

Following the directions on his GPS, Austin ended up at an ordinary-looking two-story house with white siding and green shutters, sheltered by rows of trees that looked to be over fifteen or sixteen feet tall. The yard looked to be well-maintained.

She'd told him that she didn't have any family, so Austin assumed she was the one taking care of her grandmother's home.

He wasn't going to disturb her this late. He wanted to make sure Bree and Emery were here.

Her car was in the driveway.

Austin released a sigh of relief. *They're here.*

He didn't park in front of the house because he didn't want to scare Bree.

Tonight, he would stay at a hotel and return tomorrow, just before noon.

Austin hoped she was willing to hear him out. He didn't know how she'd found out, but he vowed to make things right between them. He didn't want to lose her or Emery. He wanted them both.

Jordin called shortly after he checked in to the hotel.

"Please tell me that you found her."

"She's here in Roseville," he said. "I'm going to go see her tomorrow afternoon. I don't want to go to the house too early. I know Emery usually takes a nap after his lunch. I figure that's the best time to try and talk to her."

"I feel awful. I should've let you tell her when you'd planned."

"We were right to wait. She didn't know me then. If she's running now—there's no telling what she would've done back then."

"I'm so glad you found her, Austin."

"Me, too."

When their conversation ended a few minutes later, he took a shower.

Austin tried not to think of what lay ahead.

* * *

Leaving the hotel, Austin turned down a side street. Then right one block.

On the corner was an antiques store, the windows filled with colorful bottles, vases and other items. Next door a small café filled up as people poured in to escape the rain and in search of coffee.

Austin found his way back to the house without turning on the GPS. He saw the white picket fence the moment he turned the corner; he hadn't really noticed it the night before. It was a nice touch, he thought.

As he neared the house, Austin eyed the tall oak trees guarding the house.

Her car was still there.

He'd come by earlier than planned because he wanted to make sure she wasn't planning to run again.

Austin parked away from the house. He wasn't ready to face her just yet.

Coward.

He felt terrible over the way Bree found out about Emery. This was not the way Austin wanted it to happen.

Dreams were often hard to separate from reality, Austin discovered as he was slowly awakened by the alarm clock five hours later.

Before Austin opened her eyes to the new day, he stretched on the firm mattress, remembering the way Bree's arms felt around him. He missed her laughter. He missed everything about her.

"Bree." Her name escaped his lips before he could stop it.

The full impact of his situation hit him.

He and Bree might never have a future together. What would this mean for Emery?

* * *

Bree brushed her teeth and ran a brush through her hair before braiding it into a single thick rope that lay against her back. She navigated through the bathroom door, making her way to the dresser underneath a television bolted high on the wall.

She grabbed a pair of jeans, tugged them on and then tucked the ends of her yellow shirt into the waistband. Bree stepped into a pair of flats, intent on getting on with her day.

I need coffee.

In the kitchen Bree set her coffee cup down on the glass-topped table and turned her face to the window. It was still raining.

The dark, gloomy weather echoed her mood.

She closed her eyes as vivid mental images churned through her mind—nights with Austin, dancing, laughing and loving. She remembered the late-night picnic near the moonlit waterfront. Lying in bed, wrapped in his arms, his whispers promising love and other tantalizing delights.

Bree curled in a fetal position, sobbing until no more tears would come. Then she got up and made her way downstairs where she sat down in the den and watched television.

Opening her eyes, Bree steeled herself for what was to come the next day. Her tear-filled gaze returned to the window, watching as raindrops streamed down the pane.

Her life was different now.

Bree wiped her face with the back of her hand. She didn't want Emery to come in and see her crying.

After two cups of coffee, she managed breakfast for them.

She woke him up fifteen minutes later.

After they ate, Bree and Emery spent the morning with her reading to him; watching a movie and painting pictures.

When the clock struck twelve, Bree took meat, cheese and condiments out of the fridge and grabbed a loaf of bread from a wooden breadbox on the countertop. "How about a sandwich?"

Emery nodded. "Ham san'wish?"

She smiled. "I think we can do that."

Bree began stacking meat and slices of cheese on a piece of bread. For a moment she paused, watching as lightning forked across the sky.

She reached for a bottle of mustard, looked up again and saw a black SUV slowly approaching the house.

Her stomach churned with nervousness.

How could Austin have found them so quickly? She hadn't even told Jordin where she was going.

Bree picked up the plate sitting on the counter and brought it over to the table. "Here you are, sweetie. When you finish, I want you to go back to your room. Okay? You can watch the Smurfs movie. I've already put it in."

"'Kay…"

She took a deep breath and headed to the front door. Bree wanted to avoid a confrontation, especially in front of Emery.

Austin got out of his SUV when she stepped outside on the porch.

Tension radiated between them like heat from a fire.

Bree felt an instant's squeezing hurt when her eyes met his. "What are you doing here? How did you find me?"

"Sweetheart, why did you leave town without a word to anyone? We were all worried about you." His words contained a strong suggestion of censure.

"I guess we both know the answers to these questions,"

Bree stated, staring at him with burning, reproachful eyes. "You're Emery's biological father and you want to take him away from me."

"I don't deny that I want to be a part of my son's life, but you have it all wrong. Just let me explain…"

"Why not be honest from the beginning?" Her tone had become chilly.

"I should've been straight with you, but Bree, I was afraid you would panic." He paused a moment before adding, "As it turns out, I had every reason to be worried."

"Are you really trying to turn this on me?" Bree showed her disbelief in the tone of her voice.

"And for your information, I didn't run away. I came here because I needed some time to think."

"That's not what I was saying."

Arms folded across her chest, she asked, "Then *what* are you saying to me, Austin?" Bree threw the words at him like stones.

"I was going to tell you the truth, but that's when I couldn't reach you."

"Aren't you just a little bit curious as to how I found out?"

He nodded. "How?"

"I came to the law firm to see if you wanted to have lunch with me. I'd stopped by Jordin's office just to say hello and I heard you talking with her. How could you two betray me like this?"

"Don't blame Jordin," Austin responded. "She's not the one at fault. *I am.*"

"She knew about this, but she never said anything to me. I guess blood is thicker than water. You're her brother and I'm just a friend."

"Bree, can we just sit and talk? I'll tell you everything."

"We're talking now."

Austin let out a long, audible breath. "Please…"

She sat down in one of the rocking chairs. "I'm listening." Her anger abated somewhat under his expression.

He sat down in the chair beside her. "Jasmine Reynolds and I had been together for almost three years. Our relationship was tumultuous at best, but I thought I was in love, and so I stayed with her until I couldn't take any more. When we broke up, she left town and never told me about the baby."

"How did you find out about Emery?"

"She moved to Vegas with a friend. They had a falling out and Cheryl moved back home. I guess she had an attack of conscience or she wanted to hurt Jasmine—I'm not sure which, but she told me everything."

"How do you know she was telling the truth?"

"When I went home to visit my mother, I ran into Jasmine and she confirmed Cheryl's story."

"Why wouldn't she just contact you?"

"I've asked that same question repeatedly," Austin stated. "The only answer I can come up with is that she wanted to hurt me. We had a bad breakup."

"I was told that the father died before the child was born," Bree said.

"That's obviously not true. I'm willing to take a paternity test to prove it."

She bit her lip until it throbbed like her pulse. "I love Emery."

"I know that, Bree. I love him, too, and I want to be a part of my son's life. I've already missed out on so much."

Her spirits sank even lower. "Tell me the truth. Were you planning to have the adoption reversed?"

"I did," he confessed. "Bree, you are his mother. I want you in his life…please believe me."

"What I believe is that your interest in me was only

because you wanted Emery. And like you said, you were willing to do whatever you had to do to make that happen." Bree shook her head. "I just wish you'd been honest with me from the beginning."

"I admit Emery was the reason I wanted to meet you, but the time we spent together…"

She rose to her feet. "No, don't…"

"What I feel for you is real, Bree."

"I don't believe you."

"You know in your heart that I'm in love with you. I came all the way here to prove it, sweetheart."

Bree peered into his eyes and felt her knees wobble a little at the intensity of Austin's stare.

He cupped her cheek in one hand, and the heat of his skin seeped into hers, causing a flush of warmth that slid through her like syrup.

She ducked her head and slapped his hand away. "Austin, I'm going to be honest with you. There's no way I'm just going to hand over my son to you without a fight. Now, I need you to leave."

"Au'tin," Emery said from the doorway.

Bree had no idea how long he had been standing there. She'd left him in the kitchen eating before coming out to the porch to talk to Austin.

"Hey, buddy," he murmured.

Bree held back her anger, her throat raw with unuttered shouts and protests. The last thing she wanted was Austin hanging around longer, but he had a right to see Emery. She would give him a few minutes with the little boy.

She felt guilty and selfish.

Austin picked up his son. "What are you up to?"

"Playin'…"

Bree didn't say anything, just sat back down while Austin talked with his son. She closed her eyes, her heart aching with pain.

He'd shaken her more than she'd thought he would. Just being near him again had awakened feelings and emotions she was trying to ignore. She had walked into it with her heart wide open.

"I need you to leave, Austin."

"We need to talk this through."

"I can't right now. This is why I left town. I needed some space to think about everything."

"I'm not giving up on us," he said. "I know that you're angry right now, but we have to have a conversation."

"I know," she responded. "I just can't do it today."

"I'd like to spend some time with Emery."

Bree shook her head.

"I'm not going to snatch him up and run away. I'm not that kind of man. Besides, you don't need the distraction of Emery while you're trying to make sense of what's going on." He looked her in the eye. "You can trust me, Bree. He's my son and I will always put his needs first."

"Please have him back by five for dinner."

A lone tear slipped from her eye.

"Sweetheart… I'll bring him back to you. *I promise.*" Austin wiped away the tear. "I'm sorry for the way I handled this."

"Just bring him back."

Chapter 17

Bree stepped aside to let Austin through the front door. She was weak with relief that her son was back. "Mommy missed you so much," she murmured, pulling him into her embrace. "I'm so glad you're back."

"I had fun with Au'tin."

She pasted on a smile. "I'm glad. Little boys are supposed to have lots of fun."

"I want to go watch TV."

"Go ahead, sweetie."

"Thank you for letting me spend time with him," Austin said when they were alone in the living room.

Her gaze became troubled, but she said nothing more, although the small creases stayed between her brows.

"I hate all this tension between us."

No response.

Austin reached for her, but she stepped away. "I can't do this with you."

"Despite what you may think about me, I want you to know that my feelings for you are real."

"The only thing we need to discuss is Emery," Bree said in a choked voice. "Nothing else matters."

"Babe, you know that's not true."

Biting her lip, Bree looked away. She refused to get swept up in the tenderness of his gaze.

The pain of Austin's betrayal still stung. "I need to cook. I wanted to have everything ready, but I couldn't…" She'd spent the time pacing and fearful that Emery might not return.

"Why don't you and Emery have dinner with me tonight?"

"I don't think it's a good idea," Bree responded. "We're not some big happy family."

"You have to eat."

"I don't have to eat with you, Austin."

"I understand why you're upset with me and you have every right to be, but I'm trying to work things out between us."

"I'm just not sure that's possible."

"Bree, what do you want me to do? You know I'm not just going to walk away from my son. We can't just ignore this situation."

"I can't do this right now. I'm sorry, Austin." Her eyes filled with tears. "You can't possibly understand what this is doing to me."

"You're wrong, Bree," he interjected. "I understand more than you know. I was never told about my own child and when I am—I find that he's been adopted."

She silently considered his words and the anguish in his voice. After a brief pause, Bree stated, "I've been selfish. I've been only thinking of myself. I'm sorry that this happened to you, Austin, but I don't regret adopting Emery."

"We both want what's best for him."

"And what is that?" she asked. "To be ripped from my arms?"

He shook his head. "I love you, Bree. I want a life with you and Emery."

"I wish I could believe you, but I'm sorry. *I don't*."

Deep down she wanted to believe that Austin was being sincere about his love for her, but it was difficult. Difficult because she knew he would do and say just about anything to be in his son's life. She loved him, but without trust…a relationship between them would not work.

"Please don't shut me out, Bree."

"I do understand how you're feeling. What happened wasn't fair to you," she stated. "What I can't understand is why you kept this from me all this time. You had to know how this would play out. Austin, you knew what this would do to me."

"Why can't you see this as a good thing? We love each other."

"That's why you should have come to me, Austin."

"I had planned to tell you…it was the same day that you let me meet Emery. I was afraid if I'd told you then—you would've changed your mind."

"I honestly don't know what I would've done," she confessed.

"Bree, please understand. I wanted so badly to see him."

"Austin, I really need some time to deal with this. Can you please give me that?"

"Are you okay?" he asked without preamble.

Her hand pressed to her stomach, Bree eyed him. "Yes, I'm fine."

"You don't look fine."

"It's a monthly problem."

"Is there anything I can do?"

He wanted to reach across and pull her into his arms and just hold her.

Bree shook her head. "It's something I've had to deal with for a long time."

"Is it like this every month?"

"No, but I've had a couple of severe bouts of endometriosis over the last few months."

She suddenly bent over, groaning in agony.

Austin was instantly by her side, holding her close as she trembled from the pain. "Baby, I'm so sorry you have to suffer like this."

Bree continued to moan.

"Lie down, sweetheart," Austin told her as he escorted her to her bedroom. "Is there something you can take for the pain?"

She gave a slight nod.

He helped her get settled in bed. "I'll get you something to drink."

Austin left and returned with a glass of water.

"Thank you," she murmured weakly.

"Let me make dinner for you and Emery before I go," Austin offered. "I promise I'll leave right after."

"That's fine," she said after a moment. "I don't have the strength to argue."

Austin hated seeing the intense pain etched in her expression. He hated more that he was the one responsible for hurting her, which no doubt factored in the agony she was now experiencing.

As much as he wanted to try and repair the damage, Austin knew he had to give her the space she needed right now. However, he wasn't going to give up on them.

His mother was arriving in the morning. Hopefully, she would be able to get through to Bree. Maybe she could make her understand what he could not.

He retrieved a package of chicken out of the refrigerator. Emery loved fried chicken. It was also something he was skilled in cooking.

When dinner was ready, Austin walked down the hall and knocked on Bree's bedroom door.

"Come in," she murmured.

"Dinner's ready," he said. "How are you feeling?"

"My body hurts, but it's not as bad as before." She eased out of bed. "I really appreciate you going out of your way like this."

"It's the least I can do."

Bree stood up. A wave of dizziness overtook her.

"Sweetheart…"

She swayed.

Strong arms swept her up and laid her back in bed.

Bree doubled over in pain.

"I think we need to get you to the hospital," Austin said.

"Emery…"

"He'll be with me."

She was in too much pain to contest. "I feel like my pelvis is full of razor blades. It hasn't been this bad in a long time."

Tears filled her eyes.

He hugged her. "It's going to be okay, babe."

She leaned into him as another wave of pain ripped through her, causing her to cry out.

After a moment Bree uttered, "I'm ready to go. This doesn't feel right."

Austin pulled into Roseville Memorial Hospital parking lot fifteen minutes later. He signaled for someone to bring a wheelchair to the car.

"Mommy okay?" Emery asked.

"She's going to be just fine, but she needs to see the doctor."

"Mommy tummy hurt."

"Yes, sweetie. My tummy hurts, but I'll be okay."

* * *

After the doctor informed them that Bree would need to have surgery, Austin made a phone call.

"Mom, I really need your help," he stated as soon as Irene answered the phone. "I need you to come to Georgia instead of Charleston."

"Georgia? Why?"

"Bree's in the hospital and has to have surgery. I'll explain when you get here. I'm going to book a ticket for you. I'll pick you up in Atlanta and bring you to Roseville."

"I'll start packing, then. I'll see you soon, son."

Chapter 18

"Who's that?" Emery asked when they stopped in front of baggage claim at the airport in Atlanta.

"That's my mom."

"You have a mommy?"

Austin chuckled. "Yes, I do."

"You don't look like you slept well," Irene said when she entered the vehicle.

"I didn't."

"How is Bree?"

"She's still in surgery," he said in a low voice. "They found a melon-size cyst on her ovary. I asked you to come because I don't want to leave her side and I need someone to watch Emery. I thought it would be a good way for you to get to know him." He would have called Jordin, but with everything coming out about Emery being Austin's biological son, he was worried that would make things worse.

Irene nodded in understanding. This thing with Bree is really bothering you."

He glanced over at his mother. "I love her."

"I can see that."

Austin took her luggage to his car and drove back to

the hospital. The three of them sat in the waiting room for news on Bree, with Irene trying to keep Emery occupied with a coloring book.

Thirty or so minutes passed before he was called to meet with the doctor.

"The surgery went fine," he told Austin. "She's in recovery now. You'll be able to see her as soon as she's awake."

"Thank you."

"Praise the good Lord," Irene murmured when Austin relayed the news from the doctor.

"Mom, the way she suffered... I've never seen anything like it. She was in so much pain."

"That disease is a terrible one."

"I hope that this surgery helps her."

Irene covered his hand with her own. "She'll be fine."

"When Bree's feeling better, I'd like for you to talk to her. Maybe you can reach her mother to mother."

"I don't know what I can tell this woman, Austin. You have a legal right to your son. I'm sure she knows this."

"Bree feels like I manipulated her."

"Well, you did make a mess of this whole thing," Irene uttered. "You didn't do this the right way, Austin."

He stole a peek at her but did not respond.

"Son, I know what you're thinking. I didn't handle the situation with your father right. I admit it."

"But you did what you thought was best at the time," he responded.

"I did what I felt I could live with."

"I did the same thing, Mom. I did what I thought was best. My timing was off, but I intended to tell her everything."

"Your intentions came a little too late."

"I'm aware of that, Mom." Austin didn't need to be reminded of the grave mistake he'd made. He also couldn't feel any worse.

Bree opened her eyes, her vision clearing as the fog lifted. She was in the hospital.

The dull ache in her stomach reminded her why she was here. They'd removed a cyst through laparoscopic surgery.

Austin knocked on the door. "Can I come in?"

"Of course," she responded.

When he walked in alone, she asked, "Where's Emery?"

"He's with my mother."

Panic set in. "What do you mean by that, Austin?"

"Calm down, babe. My mother is in town. I had her come to help with Emery while I was here with you. They're in the waiting room. He's been really worried about you, but I've assured him that you're fine."

She relaxed. "I'd like to meet her and I need to see my son."

"I'll get them."

He left and returned with Irene and Emery in tow.

"This is my mother," Austin said. "Irene DuGrandpre."

Emery was delighted to see Bree. "Mommy, you got a ouchy?"

She painted on a smile. "I'm feeling much better now, sweetie."

"The doctor fixed you?"

Bree nodded. She glanced over at Irene and said, "It's very nice to finally meet you. Thank you so much for coming all the way here."

Not one to beat around the bush, Irene said, "I told Austin that he handled this situation all wrong."

Bree shifted in the hospital bed. "I definitely agree."

"I'm still in the room," he interjected.

"Why don't you go spend some time with this little sweetie?" Irene suggested. "I'm sure he's hungry. I'll stay here with Bree. I'd like to get to know this young lady."

"Despite what's going on between us, I'm glad Austin was here because I never thought I'd end up in the hospital."

"He's a good man, Bree," Irene stated. "Although Austin's approach was not the right way to do this—my son wasn't being malicious."

"Deep down I know he wasn't," she responded. "He was acting out of love for his son."

"He waited to tell you because Austin wanted to see if the child was happy and if you were a good mother. Surely you can understand why he'd want to know this."

"I suppose so," Bree murmured. "I have to confess that I probably would've done the same thing. Only I wouldn't have waited so long to tell him who I was."

"My son really cares for you."

"Trust is a big deal for me," she stated. "And I don't like being manipulated. Jordin and I have been friends since college. Knowing she had a part in this really hurts."

"They were only trying to protect you."

"I didn't need protection. I needed the truth."

Irene nodded in understanding. "I kept Austin away from his father because I needed to get away from him—at least that's what I told myself. There was a part of me that wanted to hurt Etienne. I never considered that I was hurting my son."

"You think I should just hand over Emery to Austin without a fight."

"I'm not saying that at all. I think you two must find a way to work out a compromise because that child will need both of you."

"If Austin gets the adoption reversed, I'll have no legal

right to Emery. I didn't give birth to him, but I've had him since he was two days old. I can't bear the thought of losing my child."

"You love my son, don't you?"

"I do," Bree acknowledged.

"Then talk to him and work this out," Irene suggested. "Austin is not an unreasonable man."

"I know that you're right, but I'm having a hard time with the fact that he manipulated me."

"That wasn't the case," Austin said from the doorway.

"I'm going to spend some time with my grandson," Irene said as she rose to her feet. "And leave you two to talk."

When she left the room, Austin took a seat in the chair facing Bree. "I wasn't manipulating you."

"You deliberately kept the truth from me. You dated me under this cloud of secrecy—what do you call it, if not manipulation?"

"I sought to protect you."

"Unfortunately, it had the opposite effect." Bree paused a moment before continuing. "Austin, I get it. I understand your reasons for doing this, but it doesn't lessen the heartache."

"I'm so sorry."

"I blame myself," she blurted. "Your attachment to Emery...it should've been a red flag of some sort. I should have questioned it."

"You know in your heart that I would never do anything to hurt that little boy. Despite my actions, you have to know that I love you."

Chapter 19

Bree was discharged home later that day.

Irene helped her get comfortable in bed while Austin played with Emery.

She was still a little groggy from the effects of the anesthesia. "I'm going to take a nap," she said.

"You rest, dear. Don't you worry about a thing. We will make sure that little boy of yours is fed."

"Thank you for all you've done, Miss Irene."

When she woke up, three hours had passed.

Bree sat up and swung her legs out of bed. She sat on the edge for a moment, trying to summon the strength to stand. Her fingers curled into fists and she closed her eyes to shut out the pain ripping through the area where she'd had surgery.

Normally, she tried to get by without medication, but not this time. Bree picked up the prescription bottle, opening it.

She swallowed two painkillers.

Bree sat there for a moment, waiting for some of the pain to subside. Using the nightstand for support, she rose to her feet.

"Sweetheart, what are you doing?" Austin asked from the doorway.

"I need to go to the bathroom."

"Let me help you." He was instantly by her side.

She held on to his arm, allowing him to escort her to the toilet.

Austin gave her some privacy.

When she opened the door, he was waiting in the bedroom. "I'm going to sit up for a little bit," Bree announced.

Austin helped her into her robe.

"What's Emery been doing?" she asked. "I hope he hasn't been giving y'all a fit."

"He hasn't been a problem at all. Right now, he's watching a movie on TV with my mom. They took a walk earlier."

"Has he been asking for me?"

"Yes," Austin stated. "I told him you were not feeling well. He wanted to give you a kiss, so I brought him in here while you were sleeping."

"Thank you for that. Emery believes his kisses make me better." Bree smiled. "I think he might be right."

The pain began to dissipate as she gingerly made her way to the family room and sat down on the sofa.

"Why don't you put your feet up?" he suggested. "You may be more comfortable."

Bree agreed as she changed her position.

Austin covered her with a throw. "Are you okay?"

She gave a slight nod. "I'm fine."

"Mommy…" Emery rushed over to her. "You no feel good still?"

"I'm feeling much better, sweetie."

He was about to climb into her lap, but Austin stopped him by saying, "My mom made some peanut butter cookies. Why don't you go into the kitchen and get some for Mommy?"

Emery half walked and half skipped out of the room.

"You're very good with him."

He looked at Bree. "I think it must come naturally or something. When I look at him, all I want to do is to love and protect him. I would do anything for that little boy."

"That's exactly how I feel."

"It's not hard to see that we both want the same thing for him," Austin said with a subtle lifting of his brows. "We're on the same side, babe."

Bree shrugged her shoulders in resignation, then leaned back and closed her eyes.

The next day Austin arrived to find Bree up and moving about. She had insisted that he go back to the hotel with his mother instead of staying at the house with them. There were times when that independent streak in her could be both endearing and frustrating.

Bree found that the sight of him still managed to take her breath away. She stepped aside to let him enter through the front door.

He handed her a dozen red, long-stemmed roses. "Hi, beautiful. This is for you."

She accepted the gift, asking, "What's this for?"

"Just because," he said, smiling. "You look gorgeous."

An electrifying shudder reverberated through Bree as she sniffed the fragrant scent. "Thanks, and thank you for the roses. This is very sweet of you to do this."

He sat down, leaned back and fit his fingers together. "Looks like you're on the mend."

She smiled. "I feel much better."

Austin spread his hands regretfully. "I hated seeing you in pain like that."

"Hopefully the surgery will help."

"Why don't I put those in a vase for you?"

"There's one in the top left cabinet," she told him.

"Did you know about the cyst?" Austin inquired when he returned to the living room.

"No, I didn't."

He took her hand in his. "I'm glad you're okay. The thought of losing you…it was unbearable."

"Thankfully, we don't have to worry about that."

"I know things have been tense between us. Bree, the bottom line is that I love you." He pulled out a ring box. "You're already the mother of my son. I want you to be my wife. Will you marry me?"

Will you marry me? There was a time when Bree would've been excited about the idea of marrying Austin. Her gaze drifted over to the engagement ring he offered her, each flawless stone throwing off light in all directions. Her eyebrows shot up in surprise.

It was exquisite.

Nothing could compete with this ring.

"Sweetheart," Austin prompted. "Did you hear me?"

Swallowing once, she peered up at Austin, who waited above her, the possessive intent in his eyes making her ache to give in.

But she couldn't do it. "I'm sorry, I can't."

Austin looked stunned. "Why?"

"I'm looking at this practically," Bree said smoothly, with no expression on her face. "We are both in this predicament and I get it. We get married—it's a way for us to both get what we want. But the problem is that I don't want a marriage of convenience. The way I see it—marriage isn't supposed to be a business arrangement."

"I know," he responded. "It's supposed to be love and commitment forever. Bree, I want that, too." Austin's cheekbones softened as he looked away. "I want a wife who loves me as I love her. I want a life partner to share the ups and downs with, knowing that we're stronger together than apart. You are that person for me."

"As much as I care about you, the truth is that I no longer trust you, Austin."

"What can I do to prove my love to you?"

"I don't know," she responded quietly. "I've been in contact with my attorney and he advised that the first thing we need to do is to have a paternity test done. Your claim to Emery has to be established before anything else."

"I'm fine with this," Austin stated. "Afterward, I want my name placed on his birth certificate."

"I propose that we table this discussion until we get the results back on the paternity test," Bree said.

He frowned in confusion. "Why? We both know that he's my son. Babe, I'm not planning to snatch him out of your arms. I simply want my paternal rights restored."

"If the adoption is voided—I lose any rights to Emery."

"That's why we should get married," Austin responded.

"We should marry for love—not to co-parent a child. It may have been the solution for Ryker and Garland, but that's not what I want for me."

"So, you would prefer that we raise Emery together, but not as man and wife?"

"It's the way it has to be."

"Right now, I know you're upset with me, but you're not thinking clearly. Take some more time to think about this. Bree, we belong together. Our son deserves to grow up in a two-parent home." Austin's heart thudded with hope as he watched her struggle against doubt and move toward trusting him. "We love each other. Before you found out that I was Emery's father—we spoke of taking our relationship to the next level. Please give me a chance to prove that I want to be with you and not just because you are the mother of my son."

"Okay," she whispered. "I'll try."

Austin kissed her on the cheek. "Thank you."

He left to go back to the hotel to pick up his mother.

Bree had insisted on making lunch for them. "I'm not an invalid. Besides, I did all of the prep work earlier."

Although she was still upset with him, Bree still enjoyed spending time with Austin. It meant something that he'd come all the way to Georgia after them. Despite everything, her heart still belonged to him, and for a very brief moment, Bree allowed herself to consider that they might have a future together.

Seated around the dining room table, they enjoyed chicken salad sandwiches, fresh fruit and freshly baked cookies.

"Everything is delicious," Irene murmured. "You must give me your recipe for the chicken salad."

"I'd be happy to," Bree responded.

She warmed beneath the heat of Austin's gaze and her body ached for his touch, but Bree knew that she couldn't allow herself to go there.

"Mom's right. You put your foot in that chicken salad."

She chuckled. "It's my foster mother's recipe. She's won awards for it."

After lunch, they settled on the front porch to soak in the autumn weather.

"This is a lovely little town," Irene told her. "I'd never heard of Roseville until Austin mentioned it."

"That's what most people say," Bree responded. "We call it Georgia's little hidden treasure. We do get our share of tourists here. That's why you see all the boutiques downtown. We have a lake that's a very popular attraction for visitors."

"Would you like to take a walk?" Austin asked.

"Go ahead," Irene encouraged. "I'll watch Emery."

The idea sent her spirits soaring. Bree was feeling a little restless. The walk would do her good.

"Your mother is a very sweet lady. I like her," she told Austin as they walked along the dusty road.

"She said the same thing about you, too."

Austin took Bree by the hand. "I feel like I'm in a Norman Rockwell painting."

Bree laughed. "You're silly."

"I've missed this...hearing you laugh like that."

"So have I."

"Sweetheart, everything is going to be okay. I promise."

She looked up at him. "You really believe this, don't you?"

He nodded. "I do because I have faith in *us*."

Bree couldn't deny the spark of excitement at the prospect of his words, but her faith was not as strong as his. She feared his interest in her was only a result of his desire to be with his son. She wanted him to love her because he simply could not do anything else.

They walked a couple of blocks before returning to the house. Bree was beginning to feel tired. "I think I need to lie down for a bit."

When they returned to the house, his mother and Emery were outside playing with his ball.

"I'm glad you came down, Miss Irene," she stated.

She smiled. "Me, too."

"I hope you'll come over tomorrow. We can continue getting to know one another." She didn't want to be rude—she just wanted some time alone. She just wanted it to be her and Emery for the evening.

Bree walked them out to the car.

He kissed her cheek. "You need to sit down and get

some rest. You've been moving around a lot today. Call me if you need anything."

"I'll be fine," she reassured him.

"I'll see you tomorrow."

Her gaze slowly lifted to his eyes. The moment they made eye contact she was snatched into a web of heated desire.

What in the world is wrong with me?

"Son, everything is going to work out."

"You really think so?"

Irene nodded. "Bree still loves you and I know she'll do what's best for Emery."

"You're right about that. She really loves him," Austin said. "I'm not sure Jasmine could have ever loved Emery like that. She's very selfish."

"I'm glad you asked me to come," Irene stated. "I need to apologize to you for what I did. I was wrong to keep you away from Etienne."

Austin reached over and took her hand in his. "Mom, we're past all that now."

Irene was one of those people who had perfected the art of giving nothing away—expressionless face, emotionless eyes. She had her arms wrapped around herself as she talked.

"I fell in love with your dad the first time I laid eyes on him." Irene smiled. "When he spoke to me, I thought I'd melt right on the spot. It wasn't long before we were spending all our free time together. Six months into the relationship, I got pregnant."

"How did he react?"

"He was happy about the baby and insisted we get married right away. Etienne was there when we told my parents. My father was furious, but your dad stood up to him.

Things were good until we lost little Jon. That's when things changed for us. When I couldn't take the hurt anymore, I left. Deep down I thought he would come after me, but he didn't."

"Why didn't you go back?"

"My pride wouldn't let me," Irene admitted. "Before the ink was dry on our divorce papers, Etienne started parading Eleanor around town. That was the last straw for me. I couldn't stay in Charleston, so I left."

"Any regrets?"

"I shouldn't have put a wedge between you and your father." Irene wiped her mouth on a napkin. "I owe Etienne an apology."

"Maybe you should reconsider talking to Dad."

"I'm considering it."

Austin picked up two paper cups. "Coffee or tea?"

"Coffee, thanks."

He poured a generous amount into each mug, then handed one to Irene.

Despair gripped Austin. He could live with the fact that Bree was disappointed in him, but he could not live with losing her love. He could live with co-parenting Emery with her, but Austin could not live with the idea of her not trusting him. Her love and respect meant a lot to him.

But he was not going to give in to his desolation. Austin was going to win back Bree's love, respect and trust.

Austin and his mother did some sightseeing the next morning. Irene wanted to visit the lake Bree talked about.

"It's beautiful out here," she said.

Austin agreed.

The sprawling grounds of Lake Roseville beckoned to

families and featured an assortment of rustic campsites and impressive villas. They glimpsed a couple of people riding through the wooded area by horseback.

"It says that the water in Lake Roseville comes from Georgia's Blue Ridge Mountains."

"This is where Bree grew up?" Irene asked.

"She lived here with her grandmother for a short time," Austin said. "Bree ended up in the system after the woman passed away."

Irene snapped a few photographs before they left.

Next, he took her to a boutique so that she could purchase a few souvenirs for friends back home.

They drove the short distance to the house.

"You go on inside," he told his mother. "I need to make a couple of phone calls."

He called Jordin and filled her in on everything that had been going on.

"Hey, I need you to do me a favor," he said.

"What do you need?"

"I need to have a document drawn up regarding Emery."

"What do you want it to say?"

After the call, Austin stepped out of the SUV and made his way to the porch. He heard laughter coming from the back of the house and followed the sound.

He found them, together, on the ground with heads bent, pulling out weeds and depositing them in a basket while Emery played with a ball. Austin indulged himself and watched.

They were laughing and chatting. His mother said something under her breath, and Bree's laughter floated across the air to him.

He smiled in response to the happy sound. He loved the sound of her laughter. Humor chased the shadows from her eyes, reminding him of the way they used to be with one another. Austin had missed hearing her laugh.

When she spotted him, Bree gestured for him to join them.

"I didn't mean to interrupt," he said.

"You're not," she responded, a glint of humor finally returning to her gaze. "You're more than welcome to help us with the yard. Make yourself useful."

Austin turned up his smile a notch. "I was just looking at that rake and thinking that I should probably put it to use."

"I'm sure," Bree murmured.

Amusement flickered in the eyes that met his. "Emery, come help me get up the leaves."

"'Kay…" The little boy ran over to Austin. "I help."

He could feel Bree's eyes on him as he raked the yard. She still loved him; Austin was sure of it.

She handed Austin a large plastic bag. "You can put them in here."

"Thank you."

He began raking, gathering up the leaves that had fallen. When Austin neared Bree, she glanced over her shoulder and said to him, "I don't know if Emery's helping or playing."

"I think it's a combination of both."

They laughed.

"Do you have a printer here?" Austin inquired after checking his text messages.

"Yes."

"Jordin just sent you some documents in an email. I need you to print them out."

She swallowed hard, then as casually as she could manage, she said, "I'll check to see if I have them."

"What's this?" Bree asked when she returned minutes later.

"Proof of everything I've been telling you."

She read over the legal document, then looked up at him. "Am I understanding this correctly? You're not going to contest the adoption?"

"No. I just want my name on the birth certificate and shared legal custody." Austin paused a moment before saying, "I told you that I wouldn't take Emery from you, Bree."

"Austin, I wanted you to be in Emery's life," she said, "but I was afraid of losing him if things didn't work out between us."

"Regardless of what happens, we will always be his parents."

Her luminous eyes widened in astonishment. "Thank you for this."

"It was the right thing to do."

Bree wrapped her arms around him. "I can't put into words what this means to me, Austin. I was so afraid of losing my son. I should've trusted you."

"It's in the past," he responded. "Let's just move forward."

She and Austin took an afternoon stroll after lunch. This time Bree took him in another direction.

"I want to show you something." They crossed the street and stood in front of the steps of a church, staring up at the arched doorways and boarded-up windows. "St. Matthew's…this is where my grandmother used to go to church. This building closed down a few years ago. They used to rent the house for guest pastors."

"Why did they close?"

"The pastor died and I guess they just couldn't get

it together after his death." After a moment, she said, "Austin…"

He looked at Bree. "Yes."

"You look like you have something on your mind. Is everything okay?"

"Everything's fine," Austin responded. "I just want this tension between us gone for good."

She took his hand in her own. "I told you that I would try and I meant it. What you did for me today…this helps a lot."

"I miss the way we used to be."

"So do I," Bree confessed.

Austin checked his watch. "We should head back. It's almost time to take Mom to the airport."

That evening they made the trip to Atlanta.

He glanced into the rearview mirror and smiled. His mother and Emery were both napping.

"I think they were asleep before we left Roseville." Bree reached over and gave his hand a light squeeze. "I really enjoyed spending time with your mother."

At the airport Irene gave Austin a hug and whispered, "You need to marry this girl. She's the one for you."

Emery and Bree said their farewells.

On the way back to Roseville, Austin thought about his mother's words. For the past couple of days, he had been thinking more and more about marriage. There was no doubt in his mind.

Austin wanted to marry Bree. Not because she was the mother of his son, but because he loved her more than life itself.

But how could he convince Bree of this?

Chapter 20

The next morning Bree and Emery met Austin at the hotel for breakfast.

"Something's come up with one of my clients," he announced. "I'd planned to stay until the weekend, but I have to leave after we eat."

"Then Emery and I are leaving, as well," she responded. "It's time for us to go home. If you give me an hour, I can pack and be ready to go."

"I can do that."

They finished eating and went to their cars.

Austin followed Bree to the house.

He packed up Emery's things while she emptied out the refrigerator.

Bree moved quickly through the house.

An hour later they were ready to leave.

"So, what happens now?" Austin asked as he carried a sleeping Emery into Bree's house in Charleston. They had been on the road for several hours. He was glad to be back.

"We have the paternity test done and make it official," Bree stated.

"I still want us to be a family."

"I promise I'll think about everything you've said."

"Yes." He touched her cheek. "Our son deserves to have both parents in the home."

"*Our* son..." she repeated. "It's going to take some time for me to get used to the idea of Emery as our child."

"I understand how you feel."

Bree glanced up at him. "I suppose you do in some way."

He looked at Emery. "When do we tell him?"

"Once we're back on solid ground."

Austin wrapped his arms around her midriff. "I have one favor to ask of you. Please don't let this come between you and Jordin."

Bree smiled. "I'm not. I plan to give her a call later today. We'll talk it out."

"I really do love you."

She put her arms around his neck. "I believe you, Austin."

He kissed her to satisfy his burning desire and aching need to feel her lips against his own. Austin drank in the sweetness of her kiss.

Although it was Thursday, it felt more like a Monday, Austin thought as he entered his office. Most likely because he'd been in Georgia for a little over a week and this was his first day back. He shifted his position in his chair, hoping to ease the ache between his shoulder blades.

He'd spent the morning answering constant phone calls, new emergencies cropping up, and now that everything had been taken care of, he dropped into his chair.

Austin breathed in the calm, hoping it wasn't the lull before another storm.

He was tired and his nerves throbbed.

Pam, his legal assistant, knocked on his door and opened it.

"I'm sorry. I know you didn't want to be interrupted."

"It was inevitable," he responded. "What's up?"

"The files just arrived from the district attorney's office. You said you wanted them as soon as they arrived."

"That I did."

He stood, meeting Pam halfway across the spacious room, saving her a few steps.

Austin knew that she'd had the same kind of day as his, so he suggested, "Why don't you take off early? It's almost four and you worked through lunch, too."

"I nibbled on something at my desk."

"Not good enough." She was pregnant and Austin wanted to make sure she took care of herself. "Go on. You need to take advantage of any quiet time you can get. After the baby comes, who knows when you'll be able to have time for yourself."

"There's a mountain of work left fo—"

"The firm won't fall apart overnight," Austin interjected. "I insist that you go home and put your feet up."

Pam smiled. "Thank you."

His eyes burned with weariness, prompting him to press his hands over them.

Another hour passed before Austin gave in to his exhaustion, headed home and fell into bed.

He opened his eyes and checked the time. It was barely eight o'clock. He'd slept for almost two hours.

Austin went to the bedroom and stripped before stepping into the shower. Bowing his head, he let the water flow over his back.

A short time later he was dressed and in the kitchen making a dinner salad. Austin felt much better than he had earlier.

The telephone rang.

"Hello, sweetheart," he said.

"Are you busy?" Bree inquired.

"No, I left the office at five and came straight home to get some sleep. I was exhausted, babe."

"It was a rough day for me, as well."

"If you don't mind, I'm just going to stay in tonight," Austin stated. "I have court tomorrow morning."

"That's fine. It'll probably be an early night for me, too."

"Where are you?" he asked.

"I'm on my way home. I had to meet with a support group and it had just ended when I called you."

He stifled a yawn. "How about I come by your place tomorrow after I leave work?"

"I'll see you then," Bree said. "Get some rest."

Austin glanced down at the salad and sighed.

"The place smells delicious," Bree said when she entered the house.

She strolled through the tan-painted door that led into a warm kitchen, where Sara, wearing a flour-covered apron, was pulling a tray out of the oven.

"Hey, sugar. You home earlier than I expected," she said, setting the tray on a cooling rack. "Emery wanted some peanut butter cookies. I followed your recipe to the letter."

Bree set two large grocery bags on the counter. "Everything you bake comes out wonderful. I'm sure the cookies are fine."

Arms folded, Sara leaned against the counter. "We haven't talked about this sudden vacation of yours yet."

"Where's Emery?"

"He's in his room playing on that iPad."

"Austin is Emery's biological father," Bree announced.

Sara's mouth opened in surprise. *"What you say?"*

"I was just as shocked. Then I panicked. That's why I left town. Miss Sara, I didn't know what else to do."

She began putting away the groceries.

"You know that man loves you and Emery."

Bree nodded. "I believe that. I just don't like the way he manipulated me." She picked up the bag of apples and placed them in the fruit bowl. "Don't get me wrong. I understand why he did it."

"I know a good man when I see one," Sara said. "You have a good one, sugar. Focus on what's most important here. A man that loves you and your son. That don't come every day."

Bree helped herself to a freshly baked cookie.

"They're too brown, don't you think?" Sara asked. "They'll be dry."

"Miss Sara, this is *delicious*. They're perfect."

"Thanks, sugar. I'm glad you're enjoying them."

Putting away a loaf of bread in the pantry, Bree said, "He asked me to marry him, and I turned him down."

Sara gasped in surprise. "Now, why did you do a fool thing like that? That man loves you."

"I felt like he was mostly asking because he didn't want to lose Emery." Bree paused a moment, then said, "I was angry then. But after everything that's happened, I still love him."

She put away the canned goods.

"Does this mean that you two are working things out?"

Biting her lip, Bree gave a slight nod. "Right now we're waiting for the results of the paternity test so that Emery's birth certificate can be amended. Emery will become a DuGrandpre."

"If you'd go on and marry that man—you'll also be a DuGrandpre, sugar. One big happy family."

"We're taking it one day at a time, Miss Sara."

"What are you and Emery doing for Thanksgiving? You're welcome to come with me to my sister's house in Columbia."

"We're actually going to have dinner with Austin's family."

"That's great," Sara said. "I didn't feel too good about leaving y'all here alone."

Bree embraced the woman. "Miss Sara, you don't have to worry about me and Emery."

"Well, I do worry about you. You're like a daughter to me."

They hugged.

"I'd better get out of the way. I'm sure Austin will be here soon."

"He's not coming by tonight," Bree stated. "I think the drive back from Georgia yesterday wore him out. He's tired. I could hear it in his voice." She reached into the refrigerator for a bottle of water. "Truth is, I'm exhausted and all I want to do is crawl into my bed and sleep."

"I'll get out your hair then, sugar. I put a plate of food in there for you."

Bree walked Sara to the front door.

She was tired and felt a bit sleep-deprived, but she wanted to spend some quality time with Emery.

"Hey, sweetie," Bree said as she entered his room. "Are you ready for some cookies and milk?"

"Mommy..." He rushed over to her, wrapping his arms around her legs." Bree felt the tenseness leave her body and she became more animated. Emery was just the fuel she needed to recharge.

* * *

The following Thursday they spent Thanksgiving with
Etienne and Eleanor and the rest of the family. Austin and
Bree decided to wait on telling the rest of his family until
after the results of the paternity test came back. After settling Emery at the children's table, Austin and Bree navigated into the dining room, where the others had gathered.

He pulled out a chair for her.

After she was seated, Austin sat down in the empty
one beside her. He didn't say anything as he listened to
the easy camaraderie between his family.

Etienne blessed the food.

"Amen," they all said in unison.

Austin handed her a plate of hot yeast rolls. "Aunt Rochelle made these from scratch. I have to warn you—you
can't eat just one."

"I'll try and restrain myself," Bree responded with a
chuckle. "I intend to leave some room for dessert."

Surrounded by the chatter of family, Austin's thoughts
landed on his mother. He couldn't help but wonder how
she was faring on this day. For many years, it was just
the two of them and a few close family members during
the holidays.

"Are you okay?"

He could feel the heat of Bree's penetrating gaze on
him and glanced over at her. "I was just thinking about
my mom."

"Have you spoken to her?"

"I called her earlier but she was at work. I'll call her
after we leave here." Austin gave her a tiny smile before
returning his attention to his plate.

He reached for the macaroni and cheese and spooned
some onto his plate. Austin then picked up the platter piled

high with ham, and placed a couple of thin slices on his plate.

Bree reached over, squeezing his hand.

After the entrée and before dessert was served, Etienne stood up to make a toast.

Austin excused himself moments later to check on Emery. He found the children laughing and teasing each other.

Emery spotted him and waved. "I have fun."

"Finish up your corn, buddy."

"Okay…"

"Did he eat all of his food?" Bree asked when Austin returned to his seat.

"He's finishing off his corn now."

That evening when they returned to Bree's house, he helped Emery get into his pajamas.

"Au'tin, I can do it," he fussed.

"Okay," he said. "I was only trying to help you, but I see that you're a big boy."

Emery grinned. "I'm big boy, Au'tin."

He heard footsteps and looked up to see Bree enter the bedroom. "He dressed himself," Austin told her.

"I'm so proud of you, sweetie."

"Me, too, Mommy."

They stayed in the bedroom with Emery until he fell asleep, and then tiptoed into the hallway.

Austin wrapped an arm around her. "I'm in the mood for a movie. How about you?"

"It's my turn to pick what we watch."

"No, it's not," he countered. "You picked that last movie, which was boring. It's my turn."

Bree turned to face him. "I'll be your best friend if you let me choose."

"That only works with Emery."

She laughed. "Hey, it was worth a shot."

In the family room, Austin placed a call to his mother, but didn't get an answer. He left a message for her.

He returned his attention to Bree and the movie they were about to watch.

"You still can't reach your mom?"

He shook his head. "I'm going to try her again when I leave here. If I can't get her then… I'm flying to Dallas to find out what's going on."

Irene called him back an hour later.

"Mom, where have you been?" he asked.

"I was out with a friend. Honey, I'm fine."

He reached over and gave Bree's hand a gentle squeeze. "I'm glad you're okay."

She snuggled against him.

Austin talked to his mother another ten minutes, then hung up.

"Now that we know your mom's okay, we can focus on each other."

He kissed her.

"You're welcome to stay here tonight," Bree said.

He normally spent the night whenever Emery wasn't home. "I need to get an early start on Christmas shopping. I'm actually going to the mall when I leave here."

"You're a brave soul," she responded, walking him to the door. "I don't have the energy to fight through the crowds. In fact, I'm making most of my purchases online."

Bree released a small moan when Austin's mouth drifted across hers, and for a moment she softened in his arms, her fingers trembling against his chest.

Austin pulled away and looked down at her tenderly. "I love you so much." As his lips touched hers once more, it was like oxygen to a fire that had been smoldering for years, but now blazed into a raging wildfire.

Desire overtaking them, Austin and Bree retreated to her bedroom, where he freed her of all clothing.

Bree couldn't hold back a shiver at the torrent of sensation pouring through her.

He paused, concern evident on his face. "Are you cold?"

"No," she murmured. "Everything is perfect."

Bree reached for his face, drawing him closer to her, and kissing him fiercely.

Austin groaned and responded with the same hunger, his mouth tangling with hers, his hands exploring her curves. He clutched at her, pressing close even as Bree pulled him closer still.

It wasn't enough for either of them.

Heart racing, breath ragged, he couldn't think of anything other than being with this amazing woman—his soul mate.

Mail in one hand and a shopping bag filled with wrapped gifts in the other, Austin was looking forward to spending his first Christmas with Bree and Emery. He dropped the gifts near a stack of presents, then scanned through the stack of envelopes in his other hand. He read the label of the large manila one.

Austin tore open the envelope and pulled out the single sheet of paper. He unfolded it, and stared down at the results. Sitting in his stomach was suddenly a boulder, stony and painful. It pressed his lungs until he couldn't breathe. "Dear Lord…" he uttered. "How could this be?"

His temper flared and curses fell from his mouth. *Jasmine*. Apparently, she had been cheating on him.

It wasn't something he'd ever considered. Although it certainly explained a lot. She started to change during the last six months or so, leading to their breakup.

He still had her phone number, although he'd meant to

throw it away. Austin squeezed his eyes shut, as if willing back further tears.

"Hello."

"Jasmine, we need to talk." He spat out the words contemptuously.

"Okay."

"I need the truth from you about Emery."

He heard a soft gasp.

"W-what are y-you talking about? What *truth*?"

"I'm not in the mood for games," he stated sharply. "I know where Emery is and I know that his blood type does not match mine. There is no way he can be my son."

His words were met with silence.

"Jasmine…" he prompted.

"I'm here."

"When I saw you a few months back, why didn't you set the record straight?" Clenching his teeth, Austin was furious.

"That's why I wanted to meet for dinner, but then you called me and you were so angry… I just couldn't."

"You didn't think I'd find out?"

"I guess I hoped you wouldn't. That's the real reason I left town with Cheryl. I was scared that the baby might not be yours."

"Who is that boy's father?"

"This guy I met one night at the club. We'd had a fight and you wouldn't return my calls, so I got drunk and had a one-night stand. To be honest, I don't remember much about the guy—not even his name. I think it was William…don't think I ever got his last name. I was ashamed and I just wanted to forget that night." She paused a moment, then said, "If I was sure it was your child—I never would've left, Austin. You are the only man I've ever loved. I couldn't risk you finding out that the child you thought was yours was actually someone else's."

"Which is exactly what happened."

"You found Emery?"

"Yes."

"Is he happy?"

"He is," Austin confirmed, his voice cold and exact.

"I'm glad."

"Thank you for telling me the truth, Jasmine."

"I'm so sor—"

"Save it," he interjected vehemently. "I'm beginning to realize that I never really knew you. I don't know how you can face yourself in a mirror."

She was crying.

"You did the right thing by giving him up," he replied with contempt that forbade any further argument.

Austin ended the call and blocked her number. He knew her well enough to know that she would try to reach out to him again.

He crept down the hall like a ghost to the room he was decorating for Emery, and hovered in the doorway.

It had all been a waste of time, money and energy because he didn't have a son. The thought was like a punch in the gut to him.

Austin's eyes grew wet with unshed tears.

He picked up the football and held it close to his aching heart.

Austin dropped down to the floor, his mind releasing all the dreams he'd had for his son—all the things he was looking forward to doing—tee ball, basketball, swimming…football when Emery was older… Everything crashed down all around him. His breath came raggedly in impotent anger and he bristled with indignation.

His cell phone rang.

He glanced down at it.

It was Bree.

Austin couldn't talk to her right now. His thoughts were racing dangerously. He couldn't talk to anyone.

Chapter 21

Austin didn't go to work the next day. He stayed in the condo, wrapped in a cocoon of anguish until he figured Bree had left the office and was on her way home.

"Hey, I was getting worried about you," she said when he arrived at her door. "You haven't returned any of my calls."

"I'm sorry," Austin responded. "I just got the results of the paternity test."

She smiled. "That's wonderful. Now you can have your name placed on the birth certificate."

Austin sank down in a nearby chair. "Actually, I can't."

"I'm not sure I understand."

"Emery is *not* my son." He felt an acute sense of loss in just saying the words. "Jasmine was cheating on me and I had no idea. Now that I think about it—I guess this is why she was in such a hurry to leave town. She knew the baby wasn't mine."

His face showed no reaction, which scared her most of all. It was like someone had turned off a switch. It had to be shock. "Austin, I'm so sorry."

Tears in his eyes, he shook his head. "All this time… Bree, I love that little boy."

Austin's features filled with so much emotion that his look almost brought tears to her eyes.

"I'm so sorry." Bree tilted up his chin. "Let me help you."

He pulled her down until she sat on his lap, while the chair leaned back with a resonant creak. Bree's hands fell instinctively over his shoulders, and wordlessly he looped his hands around her hips, holding her close. "What can I do to lessen the pain?"

"Just this," Austin whispered.

She wanted to ask, but didn't want to force him to talk if he wasn't ready. Bree kissed his cheek. "Hon, everything is going to be okay."

Austin gestured for her to get up and rose to his feet. "I've gotta get out of here," he said.

"Don't leave," Bree blurted. "Please, Austin, I've never seen you like this. In your frame of mind, I'll worry about you driving."

"I'll be fine."

"Austin…"

He shook his head. "I have to go. I'm sorry."

Bree's throat closed as she watched him walk away. Shoulders squared, back straight, his dark suit, a shadow of pain clinging to him.

She continued to watch until he drove away.

Her heart ached for the man she loved. She had never met his ex-girlfriend, but imagined she was nothing but a manipulative witch. Who else would play with someone's feelings like this?

He had been looking forward to his first Christmas with Emery and now this… Bree wished that the results had not come until after the holidays. It was then she fully

understood why Austin delayed giving her the news about
Emery. He was trying to protect her in the same way he
wanted to protect him.

Regardless of what the test results said, Austin was a
father to Emery. Having the same blood did not necessar-
ily make a person family. Bree knew this from firsthand
experience.

She would give him some time to deal with the shock,
but she wasn't going to let him stay in this space. They
were going to celebrate Christmas as a family. Bree wasn't
going to accept anything less. This time she would be the
one fighting for her family.

"Bree called me," Jordin stated when he opened the
front door. "She thought you might need some company."

Austin stepped aside to let her enter. His sense of loss
was beyond tears.

They sat down in the living room.

After a moment he uttered, "You didn't have to come
all the way over here, Jordin. I'm fine."

"I don't believe you."

He met her gaze. "I feel like a fool," Austin said after
a moment, shaking his head regretfully.

"*Why?* You had no idea that you'd been given wrong
information. Jasmine's friend brought all this to you."

"I'm sure she was only going by what she was told.
Cheryl wasn't a messy person."

"I find that surprising that she didn't know Emery
wasn't your child," Jordin said. "Especially since she was
Jasmine's best friend."

Austin considered her words. "I guess you're right. I
hadn't thought about it that way."

"You told me that the last time you saw Jasmine, she
wanted to talk to you."

"Yeah," he responded. "Over dinner."

"Maybe that's why Jasmine wanted to meet you that night," Jordin suggested. "Maybe she was going to tell you the truth. She had to know that you wouldn't just walk away from your son without a fight."

"Sis, it wouldn't have mattered because I wouldn't have believed her. She's a big liar." Austin released a long sigh, clasped his hands together and stared down at them.

Jordin shook her head. "I really don't understand women like her. One thing I know for sure is that Bree loves you, Austin. So does Emery. It's not too late for the two of you to become a family."

"I'm still working to regain her trust. Things are good between us, but I don't think she's ready to accept my marriage proposal."

"You proposed to her?"

He nodded. "When we were in Georgia, but she turned me down."

Jordin smiled. "She was upset then. I'm sure you don't have to worry about that now. Unless you decide to walk away."

His eyes filled with tears. "I have no claim to Emery."

"He may not be of your blood, but you've acted like a father to that boy…how can you abandon him now?"

"I don't know what to do."

"Do what you planned, Austin. *Be Emery's father.* You love Bree and you love that child."

"I do love them."

"Then you can't give up on them."

"I think Bree's given up on me," he responded. "She values honesty above all things and she feels I wasn't truthful with her. Jordin, I have to accept my part in all this and it's cost me a great deal."

A lone tear slipped down his cheek.

"I don't believe that," Jordin murmured as she embraced him. "Bree still loves you."

"I never knew love could hurt this much."

Jordin walked into the kitchen and made him a cup of tea. She brought the mug to him.

"Thank you, sis."

"I know it doesn't feel like it right now, but everything is going to work out between you and Bree. You're not going to lose your family."

Austin sipped the hot liquid. "I love them both more than my own life, sis. There was so much I wanted to do with that boy."

"And you can still do those things. Does finding out that he's not your son change your heart?"

Austin shook his head. "No."

"Then go to Bree," Jordin advised. "Let her know that you still want to be Emery's father and her husband."

Bree did not rest well. Her thoughts all night had been consumed with Austin and the pain he was going through.

After breakfast, she called to check on him. "How are you?"

"Still a bit numb," he responded.

"You know how you always tell me that things are going to work out fine," Bree began. "Well, you have to believe that this is going to be okay."

"Yeah," was his response.

"Are you going to the office today?"

"Yeah," he answered. "I need to keep busy."

"Honey, I hate the hurt I hear in your voice," Bree said. "I'm so sorry."

"Don't worry about me. I'll be fine."

She didn't believe his words any more than Austin believed them. She knew he was trying not to fall apart with her.

"I need to get going," he said. "I'll talk to you later."

Bree decided she was going to surprise Austin by taking him to lunch. She had to do something to cheer him up. *I need to remind him of how important he is to Emery.*

She walked through the Broad Street entrance of the building that housed the law firm a few minutes after 1 p.m. Bree knew that Austin never went to lunch before then.

She called him from the reception area. "Hey, I'm here."

"This is a surprise."

"I'd like to take you to lunch."

"Would you now…" he murmured.

Bree smiled. He almost sounded like his old self. "You probably need to eat something. I'm pretty sure you haven't left your office much since you got here."

"Sometimes I forget how well you know me. I'll be right out."

Minutes later he strode through a door. She met him halfway. "Hey, handsome."

"Where are we going?" Austin asked.

"Wherever you'd like to go."

They walked out of the building.

Out the corner of her eye, Bree saw a young woman getting out of a black town car. She wouldn't have paid her any mind, but Austin had a violent moment of reaction to seeing the woman, which she recognized as anger.

The woman was eyeing her, curiosity coloring her expression.

He stopped walking as she neared and asked, "Jasmine, why did you come here?"

Bree felt a thread of apprehension. What was Emery's biological mother doing in Charleston? She glanced up at Austin.

His expression was clouded with fury.

"I came to see you because I didn't like the way we ended our conversation. I'd like to speak to you *alone*."

"I'm not going anywhere," Bree stated.

"And you are *who*?" she asked, looking down her nose. "Actually, it doesn't even matter. This has nothing to do with you."

"That's where you're wrong," Austin replied sharply, taking Bree's hand in his own. "This is Emery's mother."

Jasmine's expression was one of pure shock. She tried to recover but was failing miserably. "You're dating the w-woman who *adopted* my s-son."

Austin's lips thinned to a furious scowl. "Our relationship is not your business."

"Does she know everything?"

Austin nodded. "Yes, she does. We don't have any secrets between us."

"Would you like to see a picture of Emery?" Bree interjected.

Jasmine's eyes filled with tears. "Yes."

She handed her a photo.

"He looks very happy and loved." Jasmine gave Bree a small smile. "Thank you for taking such good care of my son."

"I love him. I can't see my life without Emery in it."

"You were made to be a mother," Jasmine stated. "I don't have those maternal instincts. I'm sure you must think I'm a horrible person."

"It takes courage to acknowledge something like that. You shouldn't hang your head in shame. You did an incredible thing—you gave your son a chance to be raised by someone who desperately wanted to be a mother, but couldn't otherwise."

"Are you planning to tell him that he's adopted?"

Bree nodded. "I want to be honest with Emery. When he's old enough to understand, I'll tell him." She glanced over at Austin before asking, "Do you want me to tell him about you?"

Jasmine shook her head. "I'd rather you didn't. I think it'll do more harm than good. Will he be able to find out my name?"

Austin shook his head. "His birth certificate reflects Bree's name. The original one with your name has been sealed. The only reason I had a copy was because Cheryl gave it to me."

"He's better off not knowing anything about me," Jasmine said. "Austin, you may not be his father by blood, but you are the one I would've chosen. Emery's very fortunate to have you both."

"He's also lucky to have had a mother who loved him enough to give him up," Bree stated.

"I guess it's time I head to my hotel."

"You're staying in town?" Austin asked.

"My husband's performing in Savannah tomorrow night. I came a day early so that I could talk to you. I'll be leaving in the morning."

Jasmine walked back to her waiting car and got inside. They watched her drive away.

"Go on and say it," Austin said as they neared her car. "I know you have something to say."

"I can't really see the two of you together. She didn't strike me as your type. She's materialistic. I could tell from her wedding ring, the designer clothes...she loves a certain type of lifestyle."

"I guess that's why we didn't work out. I prefer to save my money."

"She loves Emery, though."

"*You really believe that?*"

Bree nodded. "Not everyone is cut out for motherhood. Jasmine recognized this about herself and she did what was best for him."

"I thought all women were born with maternal instincts."

"That belief is a myth," Bree stated. "There are women who find the idea of motherhood exciting, but find that having to commit eighteen years to raising a child frightening. While women's bodies are designed to carry children, it doesn't make them mothers. In grad school, I wrote a paper on this topic. Women like Jasmine value freedom and independence over the responsibility of being a mother."

"I guess I hadn't looked at it from that perspective."

They walked into the restaurant.

Once they were seated, Bree stated, "She's still in love with you."

Austin looked up from his menu. "I don't return those feelings."

"You still feel betrayed, though."

"Are you analyzing me?"

"No, I don't have to—I can see the pain in your expression."

"Everything you and I have gone through could've been avoided if she'd just told me the truth."

"I'm glad she didn't," Bree said, "because we wouldn't have met."

"Maybe we would have," Austin countered. "My family is here and you're my sister's best friend. I believe our meeting was inevitable."

The waiter came to take their orders.

While they waited for the food to arrive, Bree said, "I hope that you're still planning to spend Christmas Eve with us. You should be there when Emery opens his presents."

"I am."

"Good," Bree stated. "It will do you both some good."

He smiled. "I believe you're right. It's just something about that little boy that makes my world a much better place."

"Emery asked me if he had a daddy."

"What did you tell him?"

"I told him yes and that he'd meet him very soon." Bree took Austin's hand. "I want you to consider adopting Emery. Then he will truly be *our* son. We can tell him Christmas Eve."

"I see you've given this a lot of thought."

"I know you love Emery. I see it every time you look at him. I hear it when you talk about him. He is the son of your heart. It was the same for me when I saw him for the first time."

"We're going to have a wonderful Christmas," Austin said. "I believe this year we will all be getting everything we want."

Bree nodded in agreement. "You're looking more like yourself now."

"I have you to thank for this early gift. *I have a son.*"

"A beautiful little boy."

Austin shook his head. "He's handsome. Girls are beautiful."

"A mother has a right to call her son whatever she wants."

He smiled. "I guess I stand corrected."

Chapter 22

The rainy night in Charleston was a perfect one for staying inside and enjoying a quiet dinner. Soft, contemporary jazz floated throughout the house accompanied by the soft patter of raindrops on the balcony.

"I've never had sushi before," Austin said, "but I'm going to keep an open mind."

"You've never tried a California roll?"

"No. Just never had a desire to try them."

"I ordered a variety for you to try," Bree announced.

"I can tell you now, if it's not cooked—I'm not sure how I'm going to like it, but what do you recommend?"

"How about the empire roll for starters? It's spicy salmon with shrimp tempura, cucumber, avocado and their house sauce."

Austin sampled it. He found the texture interesting, but not offensive. "It's not bad. Not bad at all."

She smiled.

"This is delicious, actually."

Bree pointed to another plate. "Now try this one. It's a spicy tuna roll."

Austin tried it, then said, "I'm not crazy about this one."

She grinned. "Wait until you try the baked king crab roll. I'm pretty sure you're going to love it."

Bree was right. "Okay, I think this might be my favorite."

He glanced over at her plate. "What are you eating?"

"It's called a rainbow roll. Would you like to try some?"

"I'll pass. I think I'm going to stick to the king crab roll."

Bree had ordered deep fried chicken cooked with egg and onion and served over rice as their main entrée.

After they finished their meal, Austin and Bree settled down in the living room.

He pulled her toward him and kissed her. Heat sparked in the pit of his stomach and ignited into an overwhelming desire.

Austin kissed her a second time; his tongue traced the soft fullness of Bree's lips.

She gave herself freely to her passion, matching him kiss for kiss.

"When will Emery be back?" he asked. Jordin had taken him to the movies and to visit with Amya and Kai.

Bree glanced at the clock. "In an hour."

Austin grinned. "That gives us enough time…"

"Is that all you think about?"

He heard the teasing in her tone. "I know you want me as much as I want you." Pulling her close, Austin kissed her; the touch of her lips on his was a delicious sensation.

"I love holding you like this," Austin whispered. He bent his head, kissing her neck.

Bree returned his kisses with reckless abandon.

He stepped away from her as if he was about to speak, but he couldn't take his eyes off her. He just stood there looking at the woman he loved.

She breathed lightly between parted lips. She didn't say a word, but Austin could see her desire in her gaze.

He helped her undress right there in the middle of the family room.

No words were spoken from their lips; they communicated only through their hearts and their passion.

A fire blazing and Christmas lights twinkling, Emery stood between Austin and Bree as they placed the ornament he'd made on the Christmas tree. The air was scented with spruce and spices from cinnamon-studded oranges.

Clad in a pair of Hulk pajamas, Emery announced, "Santa comin' tonight."

When that cute little boy looked up at him with big, adoring eyes and a sweet smile, Austin wanted to be the best man he could possibly be.

"I know. I bet he's bringing you a lot of presents."

"Mommy say I was a good boy."

"That's what Santa looks for—good boys and girls."

Bree sank onto the sofa by the Christmas tree while Austin put their son to bed.

"Austin, I love watching you with Emery. You were made to be a father."

He sat on the rug in front of the fire. "I still feel like he's a part of me—that he's mine."

"I never had a real family, Austin. I don't know who my father was, and I don't want my son ever feeling the way I did. He needs you. I need you."

"I need you, too," Austin responded.

"I want you to know that I'd like to adopt again. I don't want Emery to be an only child."

He smiled. "We can adopt as many children as you want, babe. But first, there's something I think we need to do."

"What's that?"

"Get married. You turned me down the first time, but I'm going to put my pride aside and ask again." Austin bent down on one knee. "Bree, will you do me the honor of becoming my wife?"

He pulled a black velvet ring box out of his pocket and opened it, revealing a cushion-cut diamond surrounded by emeralds. Beside it was a smaller ring, a simple white gold band.

"That's for Emery," Austin announced. "I'm committing myself to be the best husband and father possible. Now, I just need an answer if you can stop crying long enough."

Bree felt her throat tighten with emotion. "Y-yes," she managed between tears.

She handed a gift to Austin. "I want you to open this tonight."

"Right now?"

Bree nodded.

Inside was a framed photo of him and Emery. They were both sleeping."

"You *are* his father," Bree murmured. "In every way that matters."

He grinned at her. "Always. Merry Christmas, babe."

"Merry Christmas."

Austin pulled her down to the rug with him and his mouth again found hers.

He was the right man, and the man she loved and would love forever.

The fire crackled and the Christmas lights seemed to twinkle even more brightly.

Bree smiled, feeling her grandmother's presence, and her love.

* * *

Bree woke up to find Austin staring at her. "How long have you been up?"

"For about an hour. Merry Christmas, babe."

"Merry Christmas, Austin." She sat up in bed, pulling the covers up to hide her nakedness. Her gaze traveled to the ring on her left hand. "I feel like this is all a wonderful dream."

"It's real. We're getting married."

Bree exhaled a long sigh of contentment. "I'm really happy."

"I'm glad." He propped himself up against a stack of pillows. "I don't know about you, but I'd like to get married as soon as possible. I don't want to deprive you of your dream wedding, though."

"I had a big wedding the first time and it was mostly Caleb's family. I had friends there, but no one outside of my foster parents. I'd like a pass on that this time around. I'm good with having the justice of the peace marry us."

"How about a small, intimate ceremony with just family?"

"Don't have any."

She glimpsed a shadow of disappointment in his eyes. "How about this…we get married and then have a really nice reception for family and friends."

"That's fine."

She studied his face. "Are you sure you're okay with this?"

"I don't care how we do it—I just want to marry you."

"Then let's plan a trip to Hawaii for the three of us," Bree said. "Unless you'd rather not take Emery. We can get married on the beach at sunset."

"No, Emery has to be there when we officially start our lives together," Austin stated. "I've never been to Hawaii."

"Neither have I, but I've always wanted to go there. I think it's the perfect place for me to become your wife."

Bree eased out of bed. "I'd better shower and get dressed. There's no telling when Emery will wake up."

"Mind if I join you?"

She smiled. "I thought you'd never ask."

Austin glanced at the clock on the nightstand. It was a few minutes past 7 a.m.

By eight o'clock, they were in the kitchen preparing breakfast.

Bree was in the middle of making scrambled eggs while he was on sausage duty.

He heard the patter of tiny feet and said, "Merry Christmas, buddy. Breakfast will be ready in a couple of minutes."

"Open presents?"

Bree planted a kiss on his forehead. "After breakfast, sweetie."

"I want juice pleeze."

"There's a cup on the table waiting for you." She scooped up eggs and put them on a plate laden with two sausage links. Austin added a piece of toast before Bree carried it over to Emery.

Austin followed with plates for him and Bree.

"Did you sleep here?" Emery asked while rubbing his eyes.

Austin smiled as he sat down. "I did."

"Why didn't you sleep in my room with me?" Emery placed a forkful of scrambled eggs into his mouth.

Bree chuckled as she dropped down in the seat facing Austin.

"Did you sleep with Mommy?"

She turned to look at Austin, curious to see how he was going to respond.

"Yes."

"Daddies sleep with mommies," Emery announced. He got out of his chair and walked around the table to where Austin sat. "Are you my daddy?"

He picked up the little boy. "What do you think?"

Nodding, Emery touched his cheek. "Can I call you Daddy?"

"It would make me very happy to hear you call me Daddy," Austin exclaimed with intense pleasure. "I love you so much."

"Love you, too, Daddy."

Bree's smile broadened in approval as she gloried in the shared moment between father and son.

After breakfast, it was time to open the presents.

Emery sat on the floor surrounded by more toys than Bree had seen anywhere outside a toy store. Austin was busy putting together a railroad set and train.

She looked on, both hands resting on the head of a stuffed brown teddy bear nearly three feet high, a gift to her from Emery. Jordin had purchased it for him to give to her, and Bree loved it.

"This is the best Christmas I've ever had," she told Austin.

He met her gaze. "For me, as well. Spending it with you and Emery... I couldn't ask for anything more."

"I want it to always be this way. I want this to be *our* tradition. I know your family's big on holidays, but I like the intimacy of it being just the three of us."

"We can do that," Austin said. "I promise."

Jazz floated slowly around them.

With Emery asleep in bed, Austin came out of the kitchen with two champagne flutes. He handed one to Bree. "I propose a toast."

She smiled and held up hers, as well. "To what, handsome?"

"You."

She chuckled.

"To me?"

"Yes, to you and to me. In a couple of months, you're going to be my wife. Most of our relationship has been fun."

"Yes," she said as their glasses clinked. "It's been fun."

Austin placed his glass down and studied her. "You are so beautiful, Bree. Sometimes I can't believe you're so much a part of my life."

"You've become very important to me. I've never been loved by anyone the way you love me and Emery." Bree walked over to the fireplace.

"This has been a beautiful day, Austin. Everything's been fabulous."

He smiled at her. "Glad you approve."

"I do. Now the thing is…you have to do this every Christmas. It has to be special every year."

"I can do that."

Bree placed her head on his chest as Austin tightened his arms around her.

Moments later she lifted her eyes to his.

As if on cue, they moved closer.

"Want to dance?" Austin asked.

"I'd love to."

They moved to the music slowly.

Non-rushed.

Their bodies swayed to the rhythm, speaking a language of love.

No words were needed.

* * *

The day after New Year's, Bree invited Jordin to lunch.

"Hey, what's going on?" Jordin asked. "You sounded really cryptic on the phone."

Bree waited until her friend was seated before holding up her left hand.

Jordin's mouth dropped open in her surprise. "Oh, my goodness! Girl, that ring is *gorgeous*. You and Austin are engaged."

"Yes."

"I'm so excited for you."

"No more excited than I am," Bree responded with a grin. "I'm so looking forward to being married again."

Jordin nodded in understanding. "So, when did Austin propose?"

"It happened Christmas Eve. We each opened one present and this was mine. We're planning to get married in Hawaii." Bree paused a moment before continuing. "He even bought a ring for Emery."

"How sweet is that?" Jordin murmured softly.

"It brought tears to my eyes."

Have you and Austin thought about a date yet?"

Bree gave a slight nod. "It's going to be in February."

"That's next month. How are you going to plan a wedding so fast?"

"It's just going to be the three of us," she responded. "We want an intimate ceremony."

Jordin's smile disappeared. "Really?"

Bree nodded. "I've already had the big wedding. I'm really not interested in having another one."

"I can't believe we're going to miss out on seeing you get married, but I do understand."

"We haven't told anyone about the engagement," Jordin said. "You're the only one who knows right now."

"Do you plan on telling the family?"

"Yes. We just haven't decided when." Bree laid down her fork. "How do you think your father's going to take the news that we want to get married without the family?"

"He'll be disappointed, but I don't think Dad's the one you really have to worry about—how will Irene feel about it?"

"I'm going to let Austin deal with his mother."

"Wise woman," Jordin said with a chuckle.

"I'm so glad that everything has worked out between you and my brother. I know that he really does love you."

"I know he does," Bree responded. "He's shown me in so many ways. Jordin, when I was in all that pain while we were in Georgia—Austin never left my side. He and his mother took such good care of me and Emery."

"I wish I could've been there for you. How has it been for you since the surgery?" Jordin picked up a French fry and stuck it into her mouth.

"I haven't been in nearly as much pain," she responded, "I still have some, but it's bearable. The treatments are helping."

Jordin signaled for the check. "This is my treat."

They left the restaurant minutes later.

"Girl, congratulations again."

They embraced.

"Thank you," Bree murmured. "We do plan on having a reception here in Charleston after we get back from Hawaii. We'll celebrate as a family."

"I just want you and Austin to be happy."

Chapter 23

The wedding went off without a hitch on Valentine's Day, the weather pleasantly warm on the beach. The vows were made, the rings exchanged and the marriage sealed with a kiss.

Back in Charleston, Austin unlocked the front door to Bree's house, then picked her up and carried her over the threshold.

"Welcome home, Mrs. DuGrandpre."

Emery laughed as if it was the funniest thing he'd ever seen. "You carry Mommy."

"One day when you get married, you'll do the same thing," Austin told his son.

"Surprise..." echoed all around the room.

Bree eyed the members of the DuGrandpre family, then looked over at Austin. "What did you do?"

"Trust me, sweetheart. This is to appease my mother, who was very upset that we didn't have a wedding."

"Should I be scared?"

He laughed. "Emery is our secret weapon."

"I can't believe your mother is actually going to be in the same room as your father and stepmother."

Austin nodded. "It might be a good idea to keep them on opposite sides of the room."

"She just arrived," Bree announced, peeking out the window. "She just got out of the taxi."

He met his mother at the door. "I'm glad you agreed to come."

"I'm not gonna miss the celebration of my only child's marriage. Even though he didn't invite me to the wedding."

"We wanted it to just be the three of us, Mom. Bree doesn't have family, and that's why she didn't want anything big. So, can you forgive me?"

Irene embraced him. "Of course."

Bree spotted Sara and went over to talk to her, but caught sight of Etienne and Eleanor coming through the front door. Her gaze strayed to Austin, who appeared to be searching for his mother.

Irene had seen them enter and was headed straight toward them.

"What's your mother doing?" Bree whispered when she rushed over to Austin.

"I don't know."

He watched as Irene greeted his father with a hug, then she embraced Eleanor. The three talked for a few minutes. His mother glanced over at him and smiled before she moved on to greet the next guest.

Dinner was a more elaborate affair. The caterers had transformed the dining room, adding to the wedding decorations and producing crystal, silver, champagne, wine, hors d'oeuvres and seafood salad, salmon, baby rack of lamb and a bouquet of fresh vegetables. Dessert was a three-layer wedding cake.

Bree was drawn into a conversation with Amya, Kai

and Emery. She bit back her laughter as they talked about Barbie being able to beat up Spider-Man.

"Barbie can't fight 'cause she a girl," Emery said. "Boys fight...not girls."

Kai looked over at her and said, "Girls can fight...can't they, Bree?"

She nodded. "There's Super Girl, Wonder Woman... lots of girls are superheroes."

"But Mommy...not Barbie."

"So tell us about the wedding," Eleanor said after the wedding cake was served.

"We waited until sunset to get married," Austin said. "Emery and I stood on the beach under an arch decorated with this gauzy fabric and vibrant red flowers, waiting for my bride. She showed up, dressed in a strapless satin gown with flowers in her hair and looking stunning. I kept thinking to myself that I was a blessed man to have this terrific woman by my side."

"I'm the one who won the lottery," Bree said. "Austin is a wonderful man and a great father."

He kissed her.

The room erupted in applause.

She glanced over at Jordin and crossed the room. Bree sat down, saying, "Hon, you don't look like you're feeling well."

"I'm a little nauseated," she admitted. "Ethan wanted me to stay home, but I wasn't about to miss this. I'm so happy for you and Austin."

She eyed her sister-in-law. "Are you pregnant?"

"Yes, but we haven't made the announcement yet," Jordin said in a low voice. "We'll tell everyone at the family dinner next weekend."

"Congratulations, sweetie."

The two women embraced.

"Do you want some crackers or something to settle your stomach?" Bree offered.

"Please…"

She left and returned minutes later with the crackers and a glass of ginger ale. "Here you go. If you need to lie down for a bit, you can go into the guest room."

Jordin gave her a grateful smile. "Thanks."

"Just go to the kitchen if you need more."

Bree found her husband and joined him for the cutting of the cake.

Several hours later, after everyone had gone home, she and Austin retired to their room.

Emery had gone with Ryker and Garland for the weekend.

"Thank you for today," Bree told him when he came out of the bathroom.

He climbed into bed with her.

Bree rearranged her pillows before settling back against them. "I saw your mom and dad talking."

"It's been a long time coming. I hope they were able to finally have closure." Austin rearranged his pillows.

"Jadin's boyfriend sure is racking up frequent flyer miles," Bree commented. "Maybe he should just move back to Charleston."

"He loves working with his uncle in Los Angeles, but from what I understand, Michael's been in love with my sister for years. I know she's tried to end it with him a couple of times, but he refuses to give up on her."

"Do you think they'll work everything out?" Bree inquired.

"Yes," Austin said with certainty.

"How can you be so sure?"

"I can feel Michael's determination…all I can say is that my sister better watch out. That man is determined to have a life with her." He pulled Bree into his arms. "Enough about our family. It's time to concentrate on us."

"I love the way you think."

Austin kissed Bree, and planned on doing a whole lot more.

"You're home."

Austin embraced his wife. "Sounds like you missed me."

"What are you talking about? We've been married for six months now," she said. "And honey, I can't wait for you to leave so I can have some time to myself."

He laughed. "Is that why you're always waiting for me at the door?"

Bree gave him a playful punch to the arm. "You make me sound like a puppy."

"You're definitely not a pup, my beautiful and sexy wife."

"Don't try to clean it up now."

He kissed her. "I'm going to take a quick shower. I'll be down by the time dinner's ready."

Austin went upstairs while Bree navigated to the kitchen to check on the baked ziti.

She removed it from the oven and sat it on the stove, then called for her son. "Emery, it's time for dinner. Wash your hands, sweetie."

"'Kay..." was his response.

They sat down to dinner fifteen minutes later.

"I'll clean up," Austin said when they finished eating.

"Hon, I don't mind—"

He cut her off by saying, "Bree, you give Emery his bath and I'll take care of the kitchen." Lowering his voice, he added with a grin, "I'll meet you in the bedroom."

"A man with a plan..."

"These came today," Bree announced when he walked out of the kitchen. "Although it's merely a formality."

"What is it?"

"The final decree of Emery's adoption papers."

Now the little boy was officially what he'd always been in Austin's heart—his son.

Later that evening as they readied for bed, Bree said, "Honey, I know we've been talking about adopting another child…"

Austin met her gaze. "Have you changed your mind?" He was looking forward to expanding their family.

"No, I haven't changed my mind," Bree responded. "But we may want to put it off for a year or so."

"Why?"

"Because we're going to have a baby." She placed his hand to her belly.

Bree immediately saw surprise leap into Austin's eyes.

"I thought you couldn't have children."

"Apparently, the laparoscopic surgery removed enough endometrial tissue to give us this chance of conceiving naturally…" She slapped his arm. "Stop grinning like that. You didn't do this by yourself, you know."

"We were meant to be a family. This proves it." He kissed her. "I love you so much."

With a whoop of joy, Austin lifted her high into the air, twirling her round and round.

* * * * *

KIMANI
ROMANCE

COMING NEXT MONTH
Available May 22, 2018

#573 WHEN I'M WITH YOU
The Lawsons of Louisiana • by Donna Hill

Longtime New Orleans bachelor Rafe Lawson is ready to tie the knot. His heart has been captured by the gorgeous Avery Richards. Then the media descends, jeopardizing her Secret Service career—and their imminent wedding. But it's the unexpected return of Rafe's first love that could cost the tycoon everything.

#574 PLEASURE IN HIS KISS
Love in the Hamptons • by Pamela Yaye

Beauty blogger and owner of the Hamptons's hottest salon Karma Sullivan has been swept off her feet by judge Morrison Drake. But she knows their passion-filled nights must end. She can't let her family secret derail Morrison's ambitious career plan. Even if it means giving up the man she loves…

#575 TEMPTING THE BEAUTY QUEEN
Once Upon a Tiara • by Carolyn Hector

If Kenzie Swayne didn't require a date for a string of upcoming weddings, she'd turn Ramon Torres's offer down flat. The gorgeous entrepreneur stood her up once already. Now Ramon needs Kenzie's expertise for a new business venture. But when past secrets are revealed, can Ramon make Kenzie his—forever?

#576 WHEREVER YOU ARE
The Jacksons of Ann Arbor • by Elle Wright

Avery Montgomery created a hit show about her old neighborhood, but she can't reveal the real reason she left town. Dr. Elwood Jackson has never forgiven Avery for leaving. But when a crisis lands her in El's emergency room, passion sparks hotter than before. Will this be their second chance?

Get 2 Free Books,
Plus 2 Free Gifts—
just for trying the Reader Service!

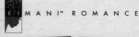

They were a natural fit with each other, as if living under
the same roof was something they'd always done. Rafe
was attentive, but gave her space. He possessed chef-like
skills in the kitchen, a penchant for neatness—she never
had to step over discarded clothing or clean up after a
meal—and above all he was a master in the bedroom and
made her see heaven on a regular basis. This man was
going to be her husband. Sometimes, when she looked
at him or held him tight between her thighs, she couldn't
believe that Rafe Lawson was hers. What she wanted was
just the two of them, but marrying Rafe was marrying
his large, controlling family.

"You sure you'll be okay until I get back from N'awlins?" He wiped off the countertop with a damp cloth.

She shimmied onto the bar stool at the island counter and extended her hands to Rafe. He took two long steps and was in front of her. He raised her hands to his lips and kissed the insides of her palms.

"I'll be fine, and right here when you get back." She leaned in to kiss him.

"Hmm, I can change my plans," he said against her lips, "and stay here, which is what I'd rather do." He caressed her hips.

Avery giggled. "Me, too, but you've been gone long enough. Take care of your business."

He stepped deep between her legs. "Business can wait." He threaded his fingers through the hair at the nape of her neck, dipped his head and kissed her collarbone.

Avery sucked in a breath of desire and instinctively tightened her legs around him. "You're going to be late," she whispered.

He brushed his lips along her neck, nibbled the lobe of her ear. "Privilege is the perk of owning your own plane. Can't leave without me."

Don't miss WHEN I'M WITH YOU
by Donna Hill, available June 2018
wherever Harlequin® Kimani Romance™ books
and ebooks are sold.

*Armstrong Black doesn't do partners, and Danielle Winstead
is not a team player. To find the criminal they're after, they
have to trust each other. But their powerful attraction throws
an unexpected curveball in their investigation!*

*Read on for a sneak preview of
SEDUCED BY THE BADGE,
the first book in Deborah Fletcher Mello's
new miniseries,
TO SEDUCE AND SERVE.*

"Why did you leave your service revolver on my bathroom
counter?" Armstrong asked as they stood at the bus stop, waiting
for her return ride.

"I can't risk keeping it strapped on me and I was afraid one of
the girls might go through my bag and find it. I knew it was safe
with you."

"I don't like you not having your gun."

"I'll be fine. I have a black belt in karate and jujitsu. I know how
to take care of myself!"

Armstrong nodded. "So you keep telling me. It doesn't mean
I'm not going to worry about you, though."

Danni rocked back and forth on her heels. Deep down she was
grateful that a man did care. For longer than she wanted to admit,
there hadn't been a man who did.

Armstrong interrupted her thoughts. "There's a protective detail
already in front of the coffee shop and another that will follow you
and your bus. There will be someone on you at all times. If you get
into any trouble, you know what to do."

Danni nodded. "I'll contact you as soon as it's feasible. And
please, if there is any change in Alissa's condition, find a way to

let me know."

"I will. I promise."

Danni's attention shifted to the bus that had turned the corner and was making its way toward them. A wave of sadness suddenly rippled through her stomach.

"You good?" Armstrong asked, sensing the change in her mood.

She nodded, biting back the rise of emotion. "I'll be fine," she answered.

As the bus pulled up to the stop, he drew her hand into his and pulled it to his mouth, kissing the backs of her fingers.

Danni gave him one last smile as she fell into line with the others boarding the bus. She tossed a look over her shoulder as he stood staring after her. The woman in front of her was pushing an infant in a stroller. A boy about eight years old and a little girl about five clung to each side of the carriage. The little girl looked back at Danni and smiled before hiding her face in her mother's skirt. The line stopped, an elderly woman closer to the front struggling with a multitude of bags to get inside.

She suddenly spun around, the man behind her eyeing her warily. "Excuse me," she said as she pushed past him and stepped aside. She called after Armstrong as she hurried back to where he stood.

"What's wrong?" he said as she came to a stop in front of him

"Nothing," Danni said as she pressed both palms against his broad chest. "Nothing at all." She lifted herself up on her toes as her gaze locked with his. Her hands slid up his chest to the sides of his face. She gently cupped her palms against his cheeks and then she pressed her lips to his.

Don't miss
SEDUCED BY THE BADGE by Deborah Fletcher Mello,
available June 2018 wherever
Harlequin® Romantic Suspense books and ebooks are sold.

www.Harlequin.com